Baseball Sleuth

Baseball Sleuth

Mark Fidler

Writers Club Press
San Jose New York Lincoln Shanghai

Baseball Sleuth

Writers Club Press
an imprint of iUniverse.com, Inc.

For information address:
iUniverse.com, Inc.
620 North 48th Street, Suite 201
Lincoln, NE 68504-3467
www.iuniverse.com

ISBN: 0-595-13044-5

Printed in the United States of America

for Bailey

CHAPTER 1

"You have a saw with you at a baseball game?" Harry asked in amazement.

Phillip looked down at Henry and his other Pizza House Brave teammates sitting on the dugout bench. "I don't just happen to have a saw with me, stupid. I told you that I figured out what they were doing. In the second half of the season, the Pharmacy Phillies have hit twice as many home runs per player as they did in the first half. Statistically, that shouldn't happen. So I figured that they must be using bats with cork in them,"

"Why would anyone put a cork in their bat?" Jamien asked Phillip.

"It's not a cork like on a bottle of wine. They drill a long hole into the tube of the fat end of the bat and slide in a piece of cork that looks like a pole. It makes the bat lighter and gives the bat more bounce. Greg Nettles did it in the major leagues. He hit a broken bat single and got caught. He was out and they fined him a lot of money."

"Really?" Harry asked. "But would a fifth grade kid think of doing something like that?"

"I heard about that stuff in the pros," Jay Rogers pitched in. "But maybe they're hitting more home runs because the pitching is getting lousier."

"I thought about that, but I don't think so. Every other team in the league has fewer home runs per game in the second half of the season. I got suspicious when the Pharmacy's hitters stopped using the aluminum bats and began using wood. There had to be a reason."

"Hey!" Coach Higgins's voice boomed as he stood in front of his team. "Pay attention to what's going on! That's three outs. Get out in the field!"

The Braves all picked up their gloves and began to walk out to their positions. Phillip, wondering what to do, stood and looked up at Coach Higgins.

"Not this inning, Phillip. I'll try to get you in next inning."

Big deal, thought Phillip. The coach *had* to put him in the next inning. The next inning was the fifth and the league rules say that every player must play at least two innings. By making it the last two, Phillip would not even play the field in the bottom of the sixth if his team was behind and didn't come back to at least tie it. Coach Higgins wasn't doing him any favor.

While the Braves were throwing the practice ball around and getting ready to play, Phillip gazed enviously at the four signed Mo Vaughn balls placed carefully on an empty bat bag at the far end of the dugout bench. Cards and Comics Superstore had just had a sale, and four guys on his team had picked up those balls at a great price just before the game. Phillip looked up as the inning started.

Phillip's Pizza House Braves were down by two in the bottom of the fourth. Jack Crawford was pitching for the Braves and doing a pretty good job. The Pharmacy only had one home run so far. Jack was behind 2-and-1 on the count when Stuart Cable of the Pharmacy smashed a grounder to Art Norton at third. Art made a great back-handed stab and threw a strike to Maggie Dwyer at first. Maggie was the only girl on Phillip's team, but she was the tallest player and could catch well, even when the balls were thrown hard. Maggie caught Art's perfect throw, and tossed the ball back to Jack. One out.

In any close game, when the Braves were home, Coach Higgins always waited until the fifth inning to put Phillip in. It wasn't fair. Even though he was probably the worst guy on the team, he wasn't that bad, and he did always show up. Phillip loved baseball, and wished he could play more. Phillip watched the Pharmacy's slugger Tao Ng (pronounced 'No') pick up one of the new wooden bats and swing it as he stepped up to the plate. Tao hadn't hit any homers in the first half of the season, but since using the wooden bats, he had put three over the fences. Phillip knew what lots of the players did this season, even in games that he wasn't playing in. Phillip lived right next to Andrews Field, and three months ago, his mom had had a baby. Since his new baby sister had come home, Phillip's mother was always either too busy or tired to do things, and so Phillip had watched a lot of baseball. He studied his team's pitcher Jack Crawford as Jack looked for the signal from Lars Crump. On the mound, Jack was tall and muscular with a graceful pitching motion. Behind the plate, Lars was pudgy and short but incredibly strong. Jack shook off the first sign from Lars like he usually did. From behind the plate, Lars flashed a different sign, and Jack nodded. Jack wound up and fired. Outside, ball one. The same thing happened the next two pitches. Three balls and no strikes. Phillip wondered whether Mr. Green, the Pharmacy coach, would give Tao the green light. If he did, Phillip hoped that Jack wouldn't give him anything too good. A 3-and-0 meatball to big Tao Ng with a cork-filled bat, well, that meant nothing but trouble.

Phillip wondered how he could test the Pharmacy bats. He had a saber saw in his baseball bag under the dugout bench. Phillip thought that a coach was supposed to file an official complaint to the umpire. No way would Coach Higgins believe Phillip and do that. Coach Higgins didn't have too much respect for

Phillip. In an earlier game, against the Firefighters, Phillip had figured out the Firefighters' signals. Phillip had told Coach Higgins that when their coach rubbed his chest and then tipped his cap, the Firefighter hitter would always bunt. The tying run had been on third at the time, and Coach Higgins didn't pull the infield in. Sure enough, the Firefighter did lay down a suicide squeeze bunt and the runner scored when Art Norton couldn't get to the ball soon enough. Even though Art was the best player on the team, he never had a chance on the play. Coach Higgins had never admitted he was wrong in keeping the infield back. In fact, he had seemed mad at Phillip about the whole thing. No way would he now believe Phillip about the corked bat.

Tao stepped out of the batters box and looked towards his coach. The Pharmacy's Mr. Green removed his cap, slowly pushed his hair up off his forehead, and put his cap back on. He rubbed his right shoulder and touched the tip of his cap. Tao nodded and returned to the batters box. Jack looked nervous. He did his full windup and pitched the ball. Tao took a massive cut. Crack! It was such a beautiful swing and such an impressive sound that Phillip forgot for a second that Tao was on the other team. So few kids used wooden bats, and a wooden bat 'cracks' instead of 'pings.' The ball shot off Tao's bat, and everyone in the park instantly knew that it would be a home run. It sailed over the center field fence. Phillip watched in awe as the ball bounced a few times and rolled all the way to the fence of the Babe Ruth diamond on the other side of the park. No one had ever hit a ball that far! The whole Pharmacy team screamed and crowded around home plate to greet Tao with high fives as he completed his home run jog.

It was now or never, Phillip thought. He grabbed the saw out of his bag, and while everyone was focusing on Tao at home plate, Phillip ran out and grabbed Tao's bat and began to saw. Back and forth, back and forth. After about ten strokes, Phillip's arm felt so tired it could hardly move. He looked at the bat. He had barely made a dent in it! He never knew that a wooden bat could be so hard.

"What's going on?" the umpire shouted.

"I challenge the Pharmacy with using cork in their bats," Phillip said with as much authority as he could muster as he wiped sawdust and sweat from the lenses of his black rimmed glasses.

"What?" the umpire asked.

"Huh?" Mr. Green of the Pharmacy uttered.

"What the..." Phillip's coach howled.

"Coach, what's your player doing?" the umpire asked Coach Higgins.

"Believe me, I have no idea, Bill," Phillip's coach said to the umpire.

Phillip continued to try to saw, but he couldn't put any muscle behind it. He was getting nowhere.

"Kid, explain yourself," the umpire said to Phillip.

"I think that they're filling their bats with cork to get more power. If you give me a chance to saw this bat in half, I can prove it to you."

"By the time you saw that bat in half, son, it'll be dark," the umpire responded.

"Please, you have to let me show you," Phillip begged.

The umpire looked towards the Pharmacy's coach. Mr. Green was a nice man and didn't know what to say.

"What do we do, coaches?" the umpire asked them both.

"I had nothing to do with this," Coach Higgins said.

"If one of my players put cork in those bats, it's news to me," Mr. Green said. "We just bought them two weeks ago. Someone stole our old bat bag, and the Pharmacy couldn't afford new aluminum bats, so we bought these wooden ones on sale. That bat is ruined now, so why don't we just finish sawing the darn thing and see for ourselves what's in it."

"Let me see those, son," the umpire said to Phillip as he reached for the bat and saw. The umpire was a very large man with huge muscles. He dwarfed the beanlike Phillip. Both teams were gathered around as the umpire sawed back and forth until the bat was in two pieces.

"Looks like wood to me," the umpire said, handing the sawed off head of the bat to Phillip.

Phillip looked at the bat end.

"Well?" the umpire asked.

"Wood," Phillip whispered.

"What do we do now?" Mr. Green asked the umpire.

"There's nothing in my book governing *this* situation," the umpire said, taking a small rule book out of his back pocket. "I guess, first, I will fine the Pizza House Braves the cost of the bat. Better yet, I'll make them replace it with an aluminum bat."

"Phillip, you're paying for it," Coach Higgins said. The umpire nodded in agreement.

"Secondly, I am ejecting Phillip from the game for unsportsmanlike conduct," the umpire stated.

"That's not fair," Juan Carlos said. Juan was the Pharmacy's pitcher and team captain. "Phillip Crafts is their worst player. He hasn't played his two innings yet, and it would *help* their team if he doesn't play. We *want* him to stay in the game!"

The big, burly umpire looked confused. The kid did have a point, his face seemed to say.

"Just a minute," the umpire said, walking away from the crowd of players and coaches. "Let me look in this book and see if I can find something." The umpire walked to first base and stood there alone flipping through the pages of his palm-sized green book. He stopped, read a little, and flipped some more pages. Once again, he stopped at a page, read carefully, and then returned the rule book to his rear pocket. He walked back to the cluster of people gathered around the plate.

"The rule book says that in cases of serious misconduct, I have the option of either ejecting the player, or forfeiting the whole game. Because I do believe that ejecting the player would actually benefit the team which committed the infraction, then I rule the game to be forfeited. Pharmacy wins."

"What!" Coach Higgins bellowed. "That's not fair! Phillip is barely on this team. He hasn't even played yet! He's more like a spectator than a player!"

Phillip hung his head in shame.

"I've made my ruling, Coach. That's the game."

The Pharmacy players all cheered, and patted Tao on the back.

Phillip was so embarrassed and unhappy that he didn't even look up at his own team. He just grabbed his glove from the bench and ran home.

CHAPTER 2

"Mom, it was terrible," Phillip whimpered.

Phillip's mother, Dara, was frantically pacing back and forth across the living room holding her wailing infant close to her chest.

"You lost, huh?" Dara asked without looking up or missing a stride.

"Worse than that, Mom. Much worse. Boy, I sure did something stupid! They lost the whole game because of me! The team must hate me and think I'm an idiot." Phillip hid his face inside his glove, trying to hold back the tears.

"You'll get better, Phillip. It just takes practice," Dara said to her son over the continued crying of the baby in her arms.

"I didn't make an error or strike out, Mom. It was worse than that. We had to forfeit the game just because of me!"

Dara noticed that Phillip had stopped talking and said, "Mike wants to help you with your game. You should give him a chance. He's quite an athlete."

Mike was Phillip's stepfather. And Mike was very serious about his sports.

"Mom, that won't help. Are you even listening to me? It wasn't my playing. I wish I had just blown a play to lose the game. This was much worse."

8

"Ooooh, that's all right," Dara almost sang to little Emily. "It's okay. It's just a little pain in your tummy. It'll get better."

"Mom, don't you even want to hear about it?" Phillip asked with pleading eyes.

Little Emily cried even louder.

"Phillip, I'm sorry. This is not a good time. We can talk later. Better yet, ask Mike to work on your game with you so this doesn't happen again. I do hate to see you upset like this." Dara continued pacing with Emily.

"Yeah, later, right," Phillip said under his breath as he got up off the couch and left the room.

Phillip stomped upstairs, stormed into his room, closed the door and lay on his bed. He stared up at the ceiling, looking right into the eyes of Tony LaRussa. LaRussa was one of the great baseball managers of the modern era. He was the first to rely on statistical analysis instead of just his gut hunches. Most kids Phillip's age had posters of the great players like Pedro Martinez, Ken Griffey Jr., or Babe Ruth, but Phillip knew that he could never play like those guys. Heck, Phillip would be thrilled just to not be the worst player on his Little League team! But Tony LaRussa was a great baseball mind, and Phillip studied baseball more than anyone he knew. Phillip believed that he could be a great manager someday. When he grew up, he wanted to be the manager of the Boston Red Sox and bring them their first World Series Championship in a very long time. But if that didn't happen, he would be a great detective. When he wasn't playing, watching or reading about baseball, Phillip was reading mysteries. And these past couple months, since Emily had been born, he had done more reading than ever.

Phillip swore that Tony LaRussa was looking right at him. He must be thinking what a dork I am, Phillip thought.

"You're right. I am an idiot," Phillip said to the poster on his ceiling.

LaRussa said nothing. He just continued to stare at Phillip.

"I bet you've never seen anything so stupid. You never would have done anything so dumb, would you?"

LaRussa just looked down at Phillip.

"I didn't think so. *You* always get all the facts and think before you act. Why didn't I do the same? Of course, there are plenty of reasons why the Pharmacy Phillies would use wooden bats. Why didn't I just ask one of their players? Half the kids on the team go to my school, and three are even in my class! Of course, a stolen bat bag does make sense. But no, I don't think of that. And all those extra home runs. There are a million reasons for that. Maybe they have a good coach who has helped them a lot. When Walt Hriniak became a big league coach, his team's hitting improved overnight. You, of all people, can appreciate the value of a good coach."

Phillip blinked and looked again at the poster. Did Tony LaRussa just smile at him? Impossible. LaRussa was no longer smiling. It was the same stare that he always gave Phillip.

Phillip finally picked up a mystery he had almost finished. It was called *The Secret of Tanager Ranch*. Phillip read two more chapters before he realized that nothing was sinking in. He was reading the words but not thinking at all about what they meant. All he could think about was a saw and a bat. And the faces of his teammates. He saw their angry faces and heard their laughter. Phillip wished that he had stayed around and faced the guys after the game and gotten it over with. He'd have to do it sometime and he dreaded it. He wanted it over and done with.

Phillip heard the front door open downstairs. It must be Mike coming home from work. He didn't want to face his stepfather. He reached over on his bed, picked up the letter he had gotten from his real father the day before, and began to reread it. After a few minutes, footsteps came up the stairs followed by a knock on the door. Phillip didn't answer.

"Phillip, are you in there?" Mike asked. "Can I come in?"

No answer.

The door opened slowly. Mike peeked in and spotted Phillip still lying on his bed.

"Can I come in, buddy?"

"Why ask? You're already in, Mike," Phillip answered angrily. "I guess there's no such thing as privacy in this house anymore." Phillip looked away from his stepfather.

"Phillip, I'm sorry about barging in, but when you didn't answer, I needed to see if you were okay. Your mother said that you made a big error or something in the game."

"It wasn't an error, Mike. Mom never listens anymore, not since that stupid baby was born. All Emily does is cry."

Mike ignored the remarks about Emily. "Tell me about the game, son."

"I'm not your son, Mike. You're my mother's husband. That's it. You don't know me or care about me at all. And if you heard what I did at the game, you'd care about me even less. I'm never going to be the baseball player you want me to be. When are you going to learn that?"

Mike's body stiffened with anger, but he took a deep breath, and remained calm. Mike sat down on the bed next to Phillip.

"Phillip, are you going to tell me about the game? I really do care."

"If you really cared, then why weren't you at the game? My real father would have been there if he didn't live in California."

Mike slammed his fist onto the bed.

"You're wrong," he exploded. "Your real father doesn't know a baseball from a golf ball. Yeah, I work hard, and I can't see all of your games. You know an electrician's hours are not regular. But I do see a lot, and I do feel bad when I miss one. Your real father could live next to Andrews Field and he'd still miss every game. Between his teaching, his research and his writing, he never saw your mother, let alone you. Why do you think your mother left him?"

"Get out of here!" Phillip screamed.

"I'm sorry, Phillip," Mike said, looking down. "I shouldn't have said that."

"Please get out, Mike. Leave me alone. I need to be alone," Phillip cried. Tears streaked down the pale skin of his face.

"I am sorry, Phillip. I lost my head. Even adults get mad and say things they shouldn't. I had no right to say those things," Mike said as he was leaving the room.

"You're right, you didn't," Phillip shot back. But everything you said is true, he thought, and he began to cry harder.

CHAPTER 3

"But Phillip, I thought that fried chicken was your favorite meal?"

"It is, Mom. I'm just not that hungry I said."

Dara and Mike exchanged glances from across the dinner table. Long, straight brown hair surrounded Dara's freckled face. Mike had short dark hair, a serious, handsome face and the solid body of an athlete. Neither said a word at first. Finally Mike spoke.

"Do you want to tell me about the game, now, Phillip?"

Phillip just shook his head no.

"Phillip," Dara said, "this is the first quiet meal we have had in a week. It's a good chance to talk as a family, like we used to do."

Dinner was Emily's worst hour. She usually screamed the whole time unless Dara fed her during the meal. But tonight, Phillip assumed, she must be sleeping. He figured that she was sleeping by the constant staticky hum of the baby monitor which his parents always had on while Emily slept. Emily's bedroom was upstairs and in the back of the house. With her bedroom door shut, you might not hear her cry from downstairs, so Mike and Dara had placed a baby monitor in the room. A baby monitor is like a walkie-talkie, but one half is only for talking into and the other half is just for listening to. Because Phillip's house was so big, Mike had gotten the strongest and most expensive monitor in the store. Phillip had been with Mike when he bought it. The guy at the store had said it was good for up to four hundred yards.

"I just don't feel like talking tonight, Mom."

Dara looked towards Mike, and Mike just shrugged his shoulders. Mike and Dara resumed their quiet eating while Phillip picked at his chicken, mashed potatoes and string beans. Phillip speared a thick green bean with his fork and began to cut through it with his dull knife. His parents got to use sharp knives, but they still made Phillip use the dull kind that are made mostly for spreading butter. They didn't realize that he was getting old. He was eleven, but they sometimes treated him like he was still five. It took about six back-and-forth motions for his knife to cut through the bean. Either it was a pretty tough bean or the knife was getting duller than ever. When he finally cut through the bean he looked into it. It reminded Phillip of the sawed through bat from the afternoon's game. No, no cork in this bean either. Actually, it had been so hard to cut through that he was a little surprised that someone hadn't filled it with metal. He could see the headline now: *Kid dies from eating a metal-filled bean. Bean maker goes to jail.* I guess that would be worse than just forfeiting a baseball game, Phillip thought. The half bean was on the end of Phillip's fork as he held it up to his eye to get a better look. Just a tiny green seed and some liquid, probably water. Phillip moved his hand, arm and fork to change the angle and get a better view.

Phillip's parents looked at him with Mike shaking his head in disgust. He began to say something, but Dara shook her head no, and Mike said nothing more. Phillip was still holding up the bean, and was now exaggerating his motions as he tried to get a better look inside. Except now he was no longer really looking into the bean. He was paying much more attention to his parents, enjoying their discomfort over how to handle the situation.

"*Eh-heh, eh-heh!*" Emily's voice crackled over the monitor. "*Waaaah!*"

"Geez!" Mike uttered in anger.

"What are you saying 'geez' for? I've had to deal with the crying all day. You just got home!" Dara snapped.

Phillip knew how hard it was on them to deal with screaming Emily. He suddenly felt bad about making this meal tough on them.

Mike continued eating.

"Mike, can you go up and bring her down? I'm exhausted," Dara said.

"Let me finish this bite," Mike garbled through a mouth full of chicken. He finished chewing, wiped the grease from around his mouth, and left the table.

As soon as Mike was out of the room, Phillip said to his mother, "Mom, I'm really not hungry. Can I be done?"

"Yes," Dara sighed.

Phillip put down his fork with the bean still on it.

"Mom, I'm going to go outside, okay?"

Dara nodded.

Phillip left through the front door just as Mike was coming downstairs with a wailing Emily in his arms. Phillip ran though his side yard, hopped over his mother's rose garden, and ran into the Curcio's back yard. In one motion he swung around the backstairs banister pole and flew up the four stairs in two pounces. Phillip knocked on the back door and just entered without hearing a response. Something smelled delicious.

"Is that you, Phillip?" Mrs. Curcio's voice rang out from the dining room.

"Yup," Phillip called back.

"Come on in, we're having dinner."

Phillip went to the kitchen cabinet and pulled down a dinner plate. As he reached into the silverware drawer for a fork and sharp knife, he heard Mrs. Curcio call, "You don't need that stuff. We're ready for you."

Phillip walked into the dining room, and Mr. and Mrs. Curcio and the three Curcio kids were all smiling at him. Even their dog, Spot, seemed to be grinning. Spot was a Dalmatian. It had been Jackson's idea to call him Spot.

"Right here, Phillip," Jackson said. Next to Jackson was an empty spot with a plate, glass and silverware already set for him.

"Jackson said that she expected you'd be here before dinner was over, and so we were ready for you today," Mrs. Curcio said, and laughed.

"You were right, Jackson, and I was wrong," Ben said to his younger sister, laughing too.

"You want some chicken pie?" Mr. Curcio asked.

"Yes, please," Phillip said as he sat down and pulled his chair in.

Mr. Curcio filled Phillip's plate with chicken pie. Phillip instantly dug in, eating everything he had. He didn't even take out the peas like he did at home!

"Phillip, I knew you'd be over after I heard about the game today," Jackson said.

"He comes for dinner almost half the time anyway these days," Ben said good-naturedly. "So you had about a fifty-fifty chance of being right anyway."

"What's a fifty-fifty chance?" Gina asked, turning to Jackson. Gina was Jackson's seven year old sister.

"It means," Mr. Curcio began.

"Howard," Mrs. Curcio interrupted, "she asked Jackson. Let Jackson answer the question."

The whole family turned towards Jackson.

"It means that half the time I might be right and half the time I might be wrong," Jackson stated.

"Do you know where the fifty comes from?" Mr. Curcio asked Jackson.

"I know," Phillip spoke out. "Out of one hundred times, fifty is half, and so fifty times she would be right and fifty times she would be wrong. Kind of like when a guy is batting three hundred-"

"Or a girl," Jackson corrected.

"Or a girl," Phillip went on. "In baseball, three hundred means three hundred times out of one thousand. Fifty-fifty means fifty out of one hundred."

"Very good," Mr. Curcio said. Mr. Curcio was a math teacher and somehow worked math into family conversations pretty often.

"Anyway," Jackson said, "I knew that you had a bad day, and you usually visit on bad days."

Jackson knew him so well. She often knew what he was thinking even when he didn't say anything. Her real name was Jacqueline Sonya Curcio, but everyone called her Jackson for short. Jackson was eleven years old, just like Phillip. She had always lived here, and Phillip had moved next door when he was four years old. He didn't remember anything from before then, though. It felt like he had always known Jackson. They were the only kids their age in the neighborhood when they were little, and they became best friends. They still were best friends. Jackson often complained that none of the girls in school liked to solve magazine mysteries, do logic puzzles or play games like chess. Phillip liked all of those things. Phillip didn't have any other friends who were girls. Most of his friends made fun of any guy who played with a girl, but Jackson was different from most girls. She was his best friend, and it seemed right. And none of the other guys really made fun of him because of it. Maybe it was because he and Jackson had always been best friends and everyone was used to it. Or maybe it was because the guys thought that Jackson might beat them up. She's not very big, but she is strong, and she's not afraid and won't back down from a fight. Probably, Phillip thought, it's that Jackson would have a way of making them feel like immature idiots if they did tease him.

"So, Phillip, is it true that you really sawed a bat in two in your Little League game?" Ben asked, wide-eyed. Ben was in high school and he seemed genuinely interested.

"Yeah," Phillip said, and even smiled a little as he thought about it.

"That's awesome," Ben said. "But I guess you were wrong. Hey, sometimes a fifty-fifty shot goes wrong."

"Seventy-thirty," Phillip said.

"What?" Ben asked.

"I gave it a seventy-thirty chance of being filled with cork," Phillip said matter-of-factly.

"Even seventy-thirty chances don't always happen," Mr. Curcio commented.

"Thirty times out of one hundred they don't," Jackson stated proudly and the whole family laughed along with Phillip.

CHAPTER 4

"So, I hear that you're quite a ball player, Phillip," Ginnie said.

Phillip shrank even deeper into the couch. Walter and Ginnie Peace were dinner guests, and Phillip's parents had insisted that he visit for a while before dinner. Ginnie had frizzy blonde hair and wore bright red lipstick. She seemed about Dara's age. Walter looked a little older, but it might have just been his balding hair and huge stomach. A beer belly, Phillip guessed.

"Oh, he's just modest, and a little shy," Dara said sweetly to her guest. "Why don't you answer Ginnie, Phillip," she said to her son in a more serious, irritated, tone.

"I'm all right, I guess," Phillip lied. He hated having to lie to adults because it was polite. Why can't people just be honest, he wondered. Phillip wanted to say, 'I stink. I'm the worst player on the team. My mom's too busy to notice and my stepfather is too embarrassed to care any more. I'm so bad that the Pharmacy begged to have me not ejected from a game when I sawed one of their bats in two.' Phillip smiled, just thinking about the reaction that his honest response would bring. His mother would kill him, though. It wasn't worth the hassle.

"I was quite a ball player myself," Walter said. "It's a great game, Phillip." Walter worked with Mike, and they were on the same softball team.

"Yes," Phillip agreed, this time honestly.

"Yeah," Walter continued, "baseball is a great game. It's a whole lot of fun, and it really teaches a guy the important lessons of life."

"Girls, too," Phillip said.

"You're right. In my day, that wasn't the case. These days you have to include girls in everything, whether they can cut it or not. I read they're even on combat ships now," Walter laughed, looking at Mike. "They didn't do that in Nam!"

Phillip's stepfather chuckled in agreement. Walter loved to talk about the war in Viet Nam.

"The only girl on our team is better than I am," Phillip said. "She plays first base, and she's probably the best fielding first baseman in the league. I don't know if she could cut it on a combat ship, but she can sure do the job on my baseball team."

"Phillip, be respectful," Dara spoke sharply to her son.

"Hey, that's all right," Walter said. "The kid has backbone, and I can respect that. He's probably right, too. Just like I was saying, he's learning important life lessons in baseball. If I had a girl who was a gold glove on my Little League baseball team, I'd feel differently about woman's issues. I'd probably be more enlightened." Walter directed this last comment to his wife Ginnie.

"Nothing could enlighten you, dear," Ginnie said kiddingly.

"I'm serious. Baseball really does teach you important things, like leadership and courage. You have to learn how to take defeat and bounce back. You learn patience. And most importantly, it prepares you for the most important thing an American adult male does, play softball!" Walter roared, and winked at Mike.

Phillip had never liked Walter and Ginnie very much. Ginnie wasn't anything like his mother. Dara would never let Mike get away those digs at women. But Ginnie always thought they were cute. Walter and Mike were a lot alike, expect Walter chose to marry Ginnie and Mike married Phillip's mother. That gave Mike a big advantage in Phillip's book. The monitor hummed in the background, and Phillip hoped that Emily would wake up and ruin their meal. At least he wouldn't have to eat dinner with these guys. Dara had let Phillip eat a frozen pizza earlier. All he had to do was to hang out for a little while before they ate.

After a few quiet seconds, Ginnie asked Dara, "So, the baby's asleep?"

"Yes, thank God," Dara sighed. "She's awfully adorable when she's asleep. You haven't seen her yet. Why don't you go up and take a peek at her? She'll never be more beautiful than now."

"Oh, I'd love to," Ginnie said. "Let's go up, Walter."

"It's the last room on the left upstairs," Dara said.

Walter and Ginnie walked quietly upstairs. Phillip nervously eyed his mother, expecting to get chewed out, but Dara seemed pretty happy and relaxed. This was the first time they'd had company for dinner since Emily had been born. Dara was in a pretty good mood.

"*Look at the baby*," Phillip and his parents overheard Ginnie say through the baby monitor.

"*Yeah*," they heard Walter respond.

"*Have you ever seen an uglier baby?*" Ginnie whispered.

"*Never*," Walter answered.

"*Turn it around and see if it has a tail*," Ginnie said.

Walter's laugh crackled through the monitor. "*Better not. They said she was her cutest when she's asleep. I'd hate to wake her and see her then.*"

They both snickered.

Phillip swallowed and looked at his mom. Dara was shaking, turning red with anger. Mike just stared at the floor with an embarrassed look on his face.

Ginnie and Walter came down the stairs.

"What a beautiful baby," Ginnie said.

More adult lying, but being polite, Phillip thought. Why can't my mom be honest now? But Phillip knew that she wouldn't be.

Dara looked away and said nothing. Phillip knew that Emily wasn't the most beautiful baby in the world. She was bald and her face was pretty red and splotchy from crying so much. But it wasn't Emily's fault. She had colic, which is sort of like a baby's stomach ache which never goes away, at least not until she gets older. Dara often talked about Phillip being a colicky baby when he was little. She laughed about it now, but Phillip knew that it had not been easy for Dara and his real dad. And so Phillip tried to not get too mad at Emily about her crying.

"I need to get dinner ready," Dara said as she left the room.

Mike did a pretty good job at pretending that nothing had happened. The men mostly talked about their softball team. Ginnie acted genuinely interested. Just as the conversation turned to the Red Sox, and Phillip began to take an interest, Dara returned from the kitchen and said, "Time for dinner."

The four adults disappeared into the dining room. Phillip just stared at the monitor. He never knew how dangerous that monitor could be, *or how valuable.* You can learn a lot about people by listening in when they don't know it. He walked over to the monitor, which lay on the side table next to the easy chair. Phillip picked it up and marveled at it. He turned one knob, and the sound of static went down. The volume knob, Phillip concluded. The knob below was labeled 'frequency.' He turned that knob and it sounded like a radio as you change stations. Suddenly he heard a voice.

"Dammit, shut up and let me watch TV," a woman yelled. *"I told you that you could stay up and watch the movie with me if you shut your mouths. Anymore noise, and you'll have to go to bed. I mean it!"*

"But she's sitting in my spot, Mom."

"She made a face at me!"

"Tell her to move!"

"She's hitting me!"

Phillip couldn't believe that the baby monitor could tune into other people's houses! These other families must own the same brand baby monitor that his parents had bought. And if they had their monitors turned on, he could listen in on their conversations without them even knowing it! Phillip smiled as he listened to another family squabbling.

"I told you, one more sound, and it's bed time!"

"Alison is younger than me. She should go to bed. And she's worse than me, too."

"She hit me with a pillow, Mom," the younger girl screamed.

"Shut up! I'm trying to hear the movie!" the mother hollered. *"Don't you want to hear the movie?"*

"It's only about grown-ups, and I don't understand it anyway. They just say bad words and nothing happens."

Phillip stared with fascination at the baby monitor as the voices went silent for a moment. He could barely hear the TV they were watching. Then he heard a faint cry. He wasn't sure whether it was from Emily upstairs or from the monitor.

"Jean, the baby is waking up," the woman's voice rang out above the background din of the television. *"Can you pop that bottle back into her mouth? Otherwise she'll make more noise than you two clods put together."*

Phillip heard the volume of the television go up, and the voices became quiet. He tried to figure out whose house he had tuned in to. Four hundred yards was a long way. It could be anywhere. Phillip barely knew the neighbors on his small street. Anyway, it didn't sound like such a great family to be part of. Maybe *his* family wasn't so bad after all. A few minutes later, hearing nothing new, Phillip turned the frequency knob.

A baby's voice was crying. That sounds familiar, and boring, Phillip thought. He turned some more. The static was thick, but a woman's voice crackled over the airwaves.

"You buried the body in the yard?"

"Where else?" a man answered.

"What if the kids find it?"

"I buried her six feet under. The kids won't dig that deep."

"Where?"

"The rose garden."

"So, what are we going to tell the girls?"

"We'll tell them that Annie had to move to a warmer climate, that she's in Florida now. They know that lots of old people like your parents do that."

"But they might ask to visit."

"They wouldn't expect that. They know that we don't have that kind of money. I wouldn't have killed her if we did."

"Did she suffer, Bob?" the woman asked.

The frequency became full of static.

"We can't let the kids find any blood," came a voice through the monitor. It sounded like the woman.

"I got it..."

More static. The voices could be heard no more. Phillip looked at the frequency. It was between 8 and 9 on the dial.

CHAPTER 5

"I suppose that you can't help me with this one," Phillip said, looking up to his Tony LaRussa poster. "You only know baseball."

It had been a day since Phillip had heard that conversation on the monitor. He'd been able to think of nothing else. The school day had been a long one. Usually, if he didn't have a baseball game or a practice after school, he went next door to Jackson's house. But Phillip wasn't sure that he should even share this with Jackson. It was so serious, and he didn't want her to somehow get into trouble over this.

"Help me, Tony," Phillip implored.

No help. Phillip looked around the room. Something was different. He was sure that he had left his closet door open this morning. Now it was closed. He was sure that he had closed the top drawer on his bureau, his sock drawer. Now it was open. Even his rug seemed to be in a little different spot. Hmmm.

He hopped out of bed, left his bedroom, and walked downstairs.

"Mom!" he called out.

"Shhh!" came the loud response from downstairs. "The baby is asleep," Dara angrily whispered as she ran to the foot of the stairs.

"Sorry!" Phillip whispered back loudly. "But Mom, has someone been in my room today?"

Dara looked nervous and hesitated before speaking. "Uh, yes. Mike went in there after you left for school this morning."

"What'd he go in my room for?" Phillip asked sharply.

"I told him he could do it, Phillip. He needed to find his saber saw. And I did see you the other day walking out of the house with it. I told him that, so he went to look for it in your room."

"Mom, what about my privacy? You've always told me that my room is *mine*. It's the one private place I have in this house! What about respecting my privacy!"

"I'm sorry, Phillip. He needed it, and besides, you took it from his work bench. Did you bother asking him for permission?"

Phillip thought for a moment and was silent.

"I guess none of us is perfect, huh?" Dara said sympathetically to her son. "And, by the way, where is it? Mike never found it in your room."

Phillip froze. The saw! He had left it at the park that day! Oh, no!

"What did you do with it?" Dara asked.

"I'm sorry, Mom. It's a long story. I hope I'll get it back tomorrow. I have a baseball game then. If I don't get it back tomorrow, I'll buy a new one with money from my own allowance."

"That's all right, Phillip. I know that you wouldn't borrow something from Mike's work table unless there was a good reason for it. I trust you. You must trust us as well. Phillip, we do love you. I know it's been hard these past few months."

Phillip nodded.

"Things will get better, Phillip. They will," Dara said gently.

"I miss doing a lot of the things that we used to do, Mom," Phillip said sadly. "You used to read to me each night. We don't do that anymore. We used to do puzzles together and play games almost every day. Mom, I miss doing that stuff."

Phillip looked up at his mother. She had tears in her eyes. Phillip suddenly felt bad about getting her so upset.

"Phillip, dear, this time won't last long. It will change."

"Will it be like it used to be, Mom?"

"No, it will never be exactly like that again."

"But I want it to be like it used to be," Phillip said, feeling ready to cry himself.

"We'll soon start to do some of those things. Once Emily's colic ends, things will settle down a lot."

"When will that be?"

"It could be tomorrow. It might be in four months. You never can tell. But, you know what? Why don't we read another chapter from *The Plains Mystery*. That was a pretty good one, if I recall."

"Mom, we haven't read a chapter in over a month. I forget what has happened."

"Okay, we can start at the beginning again," Dara said cheerfully.

"Sure, Mom," Phillip said, happy for a change.

It took Dara about five minutes to find the book. It was at the bottom of a pile of books on the floor next to the overfilled book-shelf. Dara sat down on the couch and Phillip snuggled up next to her in his usual spot. Dara opened the book and turned to the first page.

"Chapter One," she read aloud.

"Waaaaaa," Emily's voice rang from the monitor.

Dara's head dropped and she shut her eyes.

"I'm sorry, Phillip."

"That's okay Mom," Phillip said, trying to look like he meant it.

Dara got up, put the book down, and headed off upstairs.

Phillip stared at the monitor. It was the first time all day he not been thinking about it. He needed to talk to someone about the whole thing. He had heard about a murder! Who could he trust? Who could give advice that would really help? Yes, Phillip thought. He knew where to go.

Jake's Sport's Card Shop was about the neatest store in the whole city. It was a skinny little store, wedged between City Hardware and Cronin's Department Store on Main Street. There was one tall, thin window in the front of the Jake's, but it was always full of taped up signs, which made the inside of the store pretty dark, even in the middle of the day. The signs were usually notices for things like used bikes for sale, apartments to rent, and baby-sitter jobs wanted. There were also signs about new cards that Jake had just gotten in. Usually, Phillip spent about five minutes reading through all the papers and cards taped to the window, but not today. Phillip couldn't concentrate on anything but the monitor conversation that he had overheard.

And so he opened the door and stepped inside. A little bell jingled as the door slammed shut.

"Why, hello there, Phillip," a short, gray haired man said from behind the counter.

"Hi, Jake."

Jake's Sport's Card Shop was small, dark and packed with stuff. Everywhere you looked there were piles of cards, packets of new cards, and boxes of individual cards wrapped in plastic. It looked more cluttered than Phillip's room, but Jake always knew exactly where everything was.

Jake was leaning over the counter, carefully writing out a new sign on a huge piece of poster board.

"Big new sale, Jake?"

Jake looked at Phillip, and the smile disappeared from his kind face.

"No, Phillip. I'm going out of business. All the kids are going to Cards and Comics Superstore these days. I can't keep up," Jake said sadly.

"But Jake, this is my favorite store. It's the only store that I go to. I went to Cards and Comics once, and the guy yelled at me for touching a Willie Mays card. I didn't buy anything and left. I don't want to have to go there. You have to stay open!"

"I wish I could, but I just don't get the business now. I have a few regular customers like you, and an occasional one time buyer, but that's about it. Most of the kids go to Cards and Comics Superstore. They seem to have lower prices, particularly on the expensive, signed stuff. And they somehow always get a hold of the hard-to-get things that the kids ask for. I don't know how they do it, but they do. I can't blame the kids for going there. I would myself."

"But Jake, you're a much nicer guy. I'd never go there, even if the cards were for free," Phillip said.

"Thank you for saying that, Phillip. It means a lot to me. It really does. I went into this business because I like kids and cards, and not really for the money. I just can't afford to operate the store at a loss. I can't complain, though. I've had four great years. When I retired, I thought that I'd die from boredom. Then I decided to open this shop, and it's been great. I've had so much fun. Kid's like you keep me young," Jake said, and smiled.

"What will you do now, Jake?"

"Oh, I'll think of something. I certainly won't sleep and read and watch TV all day like I did when I first retired. I'll find a new project."

"Can I help you when you do?"

"If it's possible, but I can't make any promises. I might take up hang gliding or some other exotic, dangerous thing. But, if it makes sense, I'd love to have you be a part of it, Phillip."

No words were spoken for a few seconds.

"So," Jake continued, "what are you looking for today? A signed Babe Ruth card? A Micky Mantle rookie card? What'll it be?"

Phillip laughed. His parents would have to sell their house to afford those cards.

"Actually, I just had a question, Jake," Phillip said. "I need some advice."

"We have a sale on advice today. It's your lucky day, Phillip. Advice is free to kids on Thursdays."

Phillip smiled, then immediately became more serious. "Jake, what would you do if you knew that someone did something bad, really bad?"

Jake thought for a second. "Depends on who did it and how bad it was," he replied.

"Let's say it was really bad, like against the law, and you didn't know the people who did it, but they live near you."

"Well," Jake said, "first I'd make pretty darn sure that these people did do it, and then I'd call the police. That's what they're there for. I'd let them take care of it. Does that help?"

"Yeah, it does. Thanks for the help."

"Is there anything else that you want to tell me?"

"It's too dangerous, Jake. I don't want to drag you into it. But thanks."

Jake gave a wave and smiled as Phillip left the store.

CHAPTER 6

Phillip spotted his team gathering around the visitors dugout. He saw Harry and Art and Maggie. Behind them was Jamien, Danny and Justin. It looked as if about half the team had gotten there already. Phillip stood by the bushes at the entrance of Andrews Field. The diamond was down the steep hill, along the fence and by the parking lot on the other side of the park. None of the guys had noticed him yet. What would they say when they saw him? This was the first time he'd be seeing them since the 'sawed bat' forfeit. Phillip wondered what he should say to them. Should he apologize? Or laugh and treat it like a joke? Or maybe it would be best if he pretended that it never happened.

Before he had a chance to decide, Jack Crawford and Lars Crump came up behind him.

"Hey, look," Jack said, "it's the saber himself!"

"You know what they say," Lars laughed, "if you can't beat 'em, saw 'em."

"Phillip's famous now. We can make a TV show out of him. *Saber Saw, the Next Generation*," Jack added and grinned.

Phillip laughed, and then asked, "You mean you guys aren't mad at me?"

"Some of the other kids are," Jack answered. "We all were, right after it happened. Art was especially mad and he still is. He's probably the only guy who's still really mad about losing

31

the game 'cause of you. But you know Art. Baseball is his life and it's dead serious. A lot of the other guys think it's pretty funny now. All the kids on all the other teams are talking about it. You're a celebrity."

"If we were in a pennant race," Lars said, "I think we'd all still be mad. But our team isn't so great, and it was about the funniest thing I've ever seen. It was almost worth losing the game to see." Even though he was short and chubby, Lars was a pretty good player but less serious than a lot of the other kids. He was probably Phillip's best friend on the team.

"The look on Mr. Sweeny's face was great. It's the first time I'd ever seen him not sure how to call the play. He's never had to look up a rule in his rule book before," Jack said.

Phillip grinned.

"And," Lars added, "the kids all think you're weird anyway, and so they weren't really surprised. It's not like you would have won the game for us with a hit."

Phillip's smile disappeared. Lars had meant to be nice by saying that, but Phillip did not feel very good about it. He tried hard to force a smile on his face.

"What about Coach Higgins?" Phillip asked.

The smiles vanished from the faces of Lars and Jack.

"Well, uh," Jack began

"Er, well," Lars tried.

"Ah, Phillip, I don't think he thinks it's as funny as we do," Jack stated.

"He's really ticked off," Lars said. "I can't ever remember seeing him so mad."

"And he has your saw, Phillip," Jack said.

"What did he say," Phillip asked nervously.

"Not much," Lars answered. "His face got all red and he shook, and yelled, 'Where's Crafts?'"

"That's all?"

"Just a lot of swears under his breath. We weren't supposed to hear them, but we all did," Jack said. "But don't worry about him. It's not like he can bench you or anything."

"Yeah, he already plays you the least that he possibly can. And right field, too. It can't be any worse," Lars said. "Oh, and did you bring money for the bat?"

"Huh?" Phillip asked.

"Money, you know, your fine. Mr. Sweeny fined you the cost of a bat. Remember he said that you had to replace it with an aluminum bat? Those things run about thirty bucks apiece."

"Oh, no, I forgot."

"What about your parents," Jack asked. "Won't they pay?"

"They don't even know about it yet."

"Then they're about the only people in Centerville who don't!" Lars said, and he and Jack laughed.

"Let's go, guys. Coach Higgins is here, and the team's getting ready to take infield practice," Lars said.

Jack and Lars sprinted down the steep grass hill towards the field. With his short legs and round body, Lars looked funny flying down the hill. Jack's long strides were graceful in comparison. Phillip usually loved to run down that hill. You get running so fast that you can't stop. It's like your legs are running all on their own, and there's nothing you can do to even slow down. But today Phillip just trudged down the rock steps to the side of the hill. He was in no hurry to see his coach.

By the time Phillip got to the diamond, his Pizza House Braves were in the field with Coach Higgins at the plate hitting flies and grounders to them. Phillip stood near Coach Higgins, waiting to be told where to play. For about five minutes, Coach Higgins said nothing and just hit balls to the rest of the team. Finally, Maggie tossed the ball from first to Lars at the plate. The ball bounced past Lars and past the coach, landing at Phillip's feet.

"Phillip," his coach said with a phony act of surprise, "when did you get here? Why aren't you out in the field?"

"Where should I play, Coach?"

"Play right field, behind Jamien. Take turns fielding them out there."

Phillip slowly began to walk out to right field, his head hung low.

"It's the saber," Harry said.

"Saber man," a few other voices called.

"Hush!" Coach Higgins yelled. "Crafts, hustle!"

As he began to jog slowly to right field, Phillip turned back to look at Coach Higgins. Phillip noticed Art's scowl when their eyes briefly met. In right field, Phillip stood behind Jamien and watched him try to catch a fly ball. Jamien didn't move as the ball bounced two feet in front of him. Phillip's one practice play was a ground ball to right field between Maggie at first and Harry at second. He never even got a chance to try to catch a fly.

Phillip was relieved to see that the umpire was not Mr. Sweeny. Another guy that Phillip didn't know was umping the game, and he called to both teams to begin the game. As the players for the two sides sat down on their benches, Coach Higgins of the Pizza House Braves and Coach LaCava of the McDermitt Insurance Twins exchanged lineups and rosters, and each gave a copy to the umpire.

"Coach," the umpire said to Coach Higgins, "you have only thirteen names on the roster. There are fourteen players on the bench. You forgot someone."

"Ump, one of our players, Phillip Crafts, can't play until he pays a fine for destroying a bat in our last game."

Phillip thought that he saw the umpire almost smile.

"How much is the fine, coach?"

"Twenty-five dollars."

"And he hasn't paid?" the umpire asked.

"No sir," Coach Higgins said with satisfaction.

"Which one is Phillip?"

"The kid on the end of the bench. The one who looks more like a professor than a ball player."

Coach Higgins smiled. The umpire didn't. He's right, Phillip thought, thinking about his gawky, pale body and big brown-rimmed glasses.

"Son, come here," the umpire called to Phillip.

Phillip walked out to home plate and met the three adults there.

"You're Phillip?"

Phillip nodded.

"I heard about the bat. When I was in college I played with a guy who stuffed his bat with cork. He got caught. Turns out his brother played for one of the other teams. That's a trick guys can't keep quiet about. So the brother on the other team told the ump. The ump looked at the bat and saw a funny circular cut at the top. Looked like the bat had a cap on. So the umpire just pried the thing off and the guy was caught. Funny thing," the umpire said.

Coach Higgins forced a smile to his face.

"So, son, you haven't paid the fine yet?"

Phillip hadn't even been told how much the fine was until now! And no one had mentioned not playing until it was paid. But Phillip was already in enough hot water with Coach Higgins. He knew when to shut his mouth.

"No," Phillip said.

The umpire put a hand on Phillip's shoulder and said, "I'm sorry, son. You won't be able to play this game."

Phillip felt the tears well up behind his eyes, but he held them back. He didn't want to give Coach Higgins the satisfaction of seeing him so upset.

Suddenly, out of the bleachers jumped Phillip's stepfather. Mike ran on to the field and joined Phillip, the umpire and the two coaches at home plate.

"Hi," Mike greeted the umpire. "I'm Mike O'Hara, Phillip's father."

"John Winnig. Glad to meet you," the umpire said.

"John," Mike said, "I have the fine. Twenty five dollars, right?" Mike reached into his wallet.

"Right."

Mike counted out a ten and three fives. He handed them over to the umpire.

"That'll do it. Coach," he addressed Coach Higgins, "add the man to the roster. Let's play ball."

Phillip had never been so happy to see his stepfather. It didn't even bother him that Mike had called himself his father. Mike didn't seem mad or anything. But how did he know about it, Phillip wondered?

Phillip's Pizza House Braves went on and played a great game. This game, Art pitched and Jack played third base. Art threw hard, and today his control was sharp as well. He didn't have a lot of stuff, but he threw a good fastball. He walked only one batter, and most of the balls the Twins hit were fielded well by the Braves. Phillip played two innings in right field and never touched the ball. But he did get up once, and was hit by the pitch and went to first base. It was a fastball which hit him on the helmet. Everyone seemed worried, but when balls hit the helmet they actually don't hurt very much. Phillip went to second when Harry walked, and scored on a Lars single to right field. Their right fielder was as bad as Phillip. Worse, actually. He couldn't even throw the ball to the cutoff man. Phillip scored easily for what turned out to be the winning run. The team crowded around him when he crossed home plate. Baseball had never been better. Even Art gave Phillip a high five and patted his butt.

When the game ended, Coach Higgins said 'Good game' to Phillip and gave him back the saw. Mike came over to the bench, and patted Phillip on the back.

"Nice game, Phillip."

"I didn't do much," Phillip said modestly, still smiling.

"You used your head this game," Mike joked and chuckled.
Phillip laughed too.

"Mike, how'd you know about the fine?"

"All the parents were talking about it in the stands. That's about all they're talking about."

"It was a pretty dumb thing I did, huh?"

"Yeah, it was," Mike said. "But if you were right, you'd be the hero. Everyone would be saying, 'What a gutsy move.'"

"So, what's the difference between a gutsy move and a stupid one?"

"If it works, it's gutsy. If it doesn't, it's stupid."

Phillip smiled.

CHAPTER 7

"So, how'd you do?" Dara asked as Phillip and Mike walked in the front door.

"We won, Mom! And I scored the winning run!"

"And he got on base using his head, Dara," Mike added. Mike and Phillip glanced at each other and grinned.

"That's great, guys," Dara said while winding up the child-swing. Even Emily seemed to smile as she swung back and forth while the swing went click-cluck...click-cluck...click-cluck.

Phillip noticed the monitor sitting quietly on the side table. Throughout the whole game, Phillip hadn't thought about the monitor once. He couldn't avoid it now. He couldn't believe that he had actually heard about a murder on it!

"Mom, can I play with the monitor?"

"Phillip, it's not a toy," Dara said.

"Emily's not sleeping, so I thought that I'd experiment to see how far it could reach. The guy at the store said four-hundred yards. I find that hard to believe."

Dara frowned and raised her eyes sympathetically at Phillip.

"Oh, I don't know, Phillip. It really isn't a toy, and it was pretty expensive."

"And, speaking of expensive..." Mike interrupted.

"Mike," Phillip said, and with his eyes pleaded with him not to say anything about the sawed bat.

"Uh, since you know how expensive it is, I think that you can be trusted with it. You did ask this time," Mike said.

Phillip looked towards his mother.

"I guess so," she said.

"Thanks, Mom. Thanks, Mike."

Giving Mike a very grateful look, Phillip grabbed the monitor and ran with it to his room. He instantly plugged it in and turned the frequency to between 8 and 9.

"*Pooh pooh. Pooh pooh,*" a baby's voice sounded through the monitor.

"*Andrea, when are you going to tell me **before** you go. Oh, God, what a mess,*" a mother's voice sounded.

It didn't sound like the same voice, Phillip thought. But maybe it was. There was quite a bit a static.

"*Cwean me, mama,*" the baby said.

"*Since when do you give **me** the orders? Let me remind you, I'm the mother in the family.*"

"*Mama. Mama. Mama,*" the baby said, laughing.

"*Ooph, Andrea, you stink to high heaven. This looks like a three wipe job, sweetie. But I do love you.*"

After a few moments the baby cried, "*Neeew diaper, neeew diaper.*"

"*How would you like some big girl pants? I think now might be a pretty safe time. You can't have anything left after this effort.*"

"No!" the baby screamed. "*Neeeeew diaper!*"

"*Okay, you're the boss. But promise me I won't be doing this when you're in high school.*"

"*Neeew diaper!*" the baby screamed even louder.

The other woman before didn't sound this sweet. But then again, no one sounds sweet when they're talking about covering up a murder they had just committed. Phillip wished that he knew that woman's name. He remembered that the man was called Bob, but there were lots of Bobs in the world.

Phillip tried turning the dial a tiny bit. The static increased, and then stopped. There was music in the distant background. He put his ear closer to the monitor. There were some voices talking but they were too far away to understand. Suddenly, a man's voice called out, *"Girls, come in!"*

Phillip turn up the volume to the highest level. The sound of the background static went up. There were still voices talking, but they remained too quiet to hear very well. That loud voice did sound like the man's voice. And he did say 'girls.' The three things that Phillip knew about this family were that the father was called Bob, they had girls, and there was a rose garden in their yard. Oh, and one other thing. They had a dead body buried in the rose garden.

It didn't sound like he would get very much information. But this was probably the right frequency. He looked more carefully at the dial. Between 8 and 9. Lots of frequencies were between 8 and 9. It was a little less than halfway between those numbers, but more than a third of the way there. About two-fifths of the way between, Phillip concluded. 8.4 on the dial, he thought. Mr. Curcio would be proud of him. Now, all he had to do was find this house. It would be a big job to do on his own, but he didn't want to burden anyone else with what he knew. It had caused him enough pain already. No one else should have to go through that too. Then Phillip had an idea.

"Jackson, you're going to have to trust me on this one," Phillip said.

"Phillip, it isn't fair. You can't ask for my help and not tell me the whole story. You know that you can trust me!"

Jackson's big brown eyes pleaded with Phillip, but he just shook his head.

"Jackson, you don't want to know. I wish that I didn't know, believe me. Please, Jackson, this is very important and very serious. Otherwise I wouldn't do this to you. But I need your help. And I can't tell you."

Jackson sighed. "Okay, but this better be important, and you have to promise to tell me *everything* when we find this house of yours."

"Not just then, but not too long afterwards."

"Okay," Jackson agreed.

Phillip smiled. "Do you have a street map of Centerville?"

"Yeah, in our map drawer. I'll be right back."

Jackson bounded out of her bedroom, her long dark brown hair tied in a pony tail bouncing behind her as she ran. Phillip didn't really like girls, but he did find himself liking to look at Jackson. In a minute, Jackson was flying back up the stairs and into her room.

"Here, Phillip," she said, breathing hard as she lay the city street map on the floor.

Phillip studied the map for a minute, and pointed as he spoke.

"Here's where we are. The baby monitor only has a range of four hundred yards, and so if I heard this family through the monitor from my house, then their house must be within four hundred yards of here. Can we draw a circle lightly on the map?"

"Yeah, you can just use pencil. We can erase it when we're done."

Jackson reached up on her desk, grabbed a pencil and handed it to Phillip.

"We need to figure out how far four hundred yards is," Phillip said, thinking.

"We can use the key, Phillip."

"The key?"

"Yes, the map key. Right there."

She pointed to a line with hash marks in it. It said 'one mile' above it, and had markers at a quarter mile, a half mile and three quarters of a mile.

"Oh, yeah. I forgot what they called that thing. Let's see, this is in miles, but we want four-hundred yards," Phillip stated.

"A mile is 1,760 yards, remember?" Jackson said.

"Oh, yeah. And so four hundred yards is about, uh, uh," Phillip hesitated.

"A little less than a quarter of a mile," Jackson finished.

"That sounds right," Phillip said, still puzzling over the problem.

"I know it's right. Because four-hundred is one quarter of sixteen-hundred. Four times four is sixteen. So it's a little less than a quarter of 1,760."

Jackson was awesome at math. Phillip always got A's in math at school, but Jackson could think of answers to problems even before she was taught how to do it. Phillip had definitely done the right thing when he had asked her for help.

"I know what to do next," Jackson said excitedly. "I saw my father do this before. Just a second."

Jackson ran out the room and went to the top of the stairs.

"Dad, where's your compass?" she hollered.

"Bottom right drawer of my desk," Mr. Curcio called back.

"Thanks!" Jackson yelled, and ran into her parents' bedroom. She was out in a second holding an instrument that looked more like a jack-knife than a compass. It was metal, had a pencil stuck in one end and a sharp metal point at the other end. Phillip had seen one of those before. They were used to draw circles.

"I thought that you were getting a compass," Phillip said.

"This is a compass, silly," Jackson laughed.

"Then, where are the directions?"

"Not that kind of a compass," Jackson said, grinning. "This draws circles any size you want. See how you change the angle between the two arms? A big angle makes a big circle and a small one makes a small circle."

"I knew that, Jackson. I just never knew it was called a compass. Kind of a dumb name for it, don't you think? It just confuses people."

"I guess so," Jackson said. "I never really thought about it. Anyway, you line up the compass with the key, like this."

Jackson put the sharp end of the compass at the 0 marker, and opened the compass so that the pencil touched the part of the line just less than the quarter mile mark. She picked up the compass, and put the pointy end at their house. She spun the compass around and drew a circle that went almost a quarter of a mile from their house. She put down the compass and they looked at the circle.

"Wow, that's a big area!" Phillip said. It went beyond Beal Street in one direction and as far as Adams Street in the other. Phillip never knew that four hundred yards could be so far.

"I didn't think it would be this big, either. This is going to be a pretty hard job," Jackson said.

"Actually, I can't believe that the monitor really goes four-hundred yards. They always exaggerate on ads," Phillip said.

"That's true," Jackson agreed.

"So, let's just start closer to us, and work our way out. We probably won't have to go so far."

"Then we are searching for a house with a rose garden some-where, the father is called Bob, and they have at least two kids and all the kids are girls, right?"

"Right," Phillip said. And they have a dead body buried in with the roses, Phillip thought.

CHAPTER 8

Phillip looked at his watch. Ten-thirty. He was supposed to have met Jackson fifteen minutes ago. Phillip hadn't had any luck on his streets. Where could Jackson be? Maybe she had found the house and decided to snoop around a bit. Maybe she had gotten caught. These people are dangerous. You don't want to get caught by them. They're not afraid to do a guy in. Or a girl, as Phillip knew. They had killed Annie. Poor Annie. Just as Phillip was beginning to wish that he had not gotten Jackson into this, he spotted her waving to him from down the street. Phillip waved back.

As Jackson approached him, Phillip angrily asked, "Where have you been?"

"Looking for your house," Jackson snapped back.

"But we were supposed to meet here at ten-fifteen. You're almost twenty minutes late!"

"I was also supposed to cover Chestnut Street, Maple Hill Ave., and Washington Street. I was at the far end of Maple Hill when it was ten past ten. It didn't make sense for me to come all the way back here to meet you, and then have to go all the way back there to do the last part of the street. I thought that you'd be pleased that I did the whole thing. But I come back and find you all mad just because I'm a few minutes late. What'd you think happened to me? Did you think I was murdered?"

Phillip didn't answer that question, but it made him shudder. "I'm sorry. I was just worried. It was stupid. Sorry."

"That's okay. I guess it's a compliment that you care so much about me. That's what my dad says to my mom when she gets mad when he's late." Jackson looked at Phillip and giggled.

She was actually right. He did care about her and he was worried, and that *was* why he had been angry. Philip felt embarrassed and just smiled. "So, how did it go?" he asked her.

"I tried the rose garden strategy. On Chestnut, I looked in each yard for a rose garden. I found five of them. Near two of them, I spotted a neighbor, and I asked if there were little girls who lived there. One house just had two old people. The other had girls, but they were older. Just to be sure, I asked if the father's name was Bob. It wasn't. It was Leland. That's not even close to Bob. I couldn't find any neighbors near the other houses with rose gardens, so I just went to the front door at each one and rang the bell."

"You what?" Phillip gasped.

"I rang the bell. Two of the houses had people home. I asked a kid who answered one door if her dad was named Bob. She said that she didn't have a dad. At the other house, a man answered. I asked him if his name was Bob. It wasn't. It was Harold. The final house had no answer, so I explored in the back yard."

"You didn't!" Phillip blurted.

"Sure I did. There was a tool shed or something. It was unlocked so I opened it and looked inside. There were only tools there, so I knew it couldn't be the right house."

"Why not?" Phillip asked.

"Because if they had kids, there would definitely be outdoor toys in that shed. They had no garage, so they'd put them there. But there weren't any, and there were none in the yard. So that couldn't have been the right house."

"Jackson," Phillip said with exasperation. "I told you to stay off the property if you thought you found it. I said it was dangerous."

"Well, maybe you should tell me everything and then I'll know how dangerous it is."

"I can't do that. You have to trust me, Jackson."

Jackson shook her head. "I'm back safe and sound. How did your search go?"

"Not so good. I only found two rose gardens. I spotted people in both neighborhoods, and none were it."

"Phillip, I don't think that this strategy will work out so well. It'll take us weeks to cover the area like this. There must be a better way. Let's think."

"How can we get a list of people who have a rose garden? Maybe there's an aerial photo someone has," Phillip suggested.

"I doubt it. Anyway, the roses would be too small to see. What about a list of people who have little girls, or men who are named Bob?"

"That's it!" Phillip exclaimed. "There is a list like that!"

"There is?" Jackson asked.

"Yes, the nosy book. Don't you guys have one?"

"The nosy book?"

"Yeah, it's that green book that the city sells each year. It tells all the people in the city who live at each house and what their ages and jobs are. My mom calls it the nosy book because you can find out all about your neighbors in it. And it's done by street," Phillip said proudly.

"You have one of these books?"

"Yeah, don't you?"

"I've never heard my parents talk about it. I don't think that my parents are very nosy. They don't really care how old other people are. My mother always says that she can't understand why people lie about their ages," Jackson said.

"Let's go get my nosy book. That should help us," Phillip suggested.

"Okay."

Phillip and Jackson ran all the way to Phillip's house. Turning the last corner, they spotted Mike pacing back and forth on the front lawn, holding Emily in the football hold. The football hold was Mike's last resort method for settling Emily down. Mike held Emily's butt in his right hand, while she lay along his forearm, with her head by his elbow. It was like the way a football running back clutches a football in one hand while he runs.

Phillip raced past Mike, into his house.

"Hi, Mr. O'Hara," Jackson said, stopping to wait outside.

"Hi, Jackson," Mike huffed. By now Mike was jogging around the yard with a whimpering Emily still in the football hold.

Just as Jackson was getting ready to head inside, Phillip ran out with a small green book in his hand.

"What you got there?" Mike asked.

"Just the nosy book," Phillip answered.

"What are you going to do with that?"

Phillip stopped. He looked at Jackson. "Uh, just gonna look some stuff up," Phillip said.

"Like what?"

"Our teachers," Jackson said. "We're going to see how old our teachers are."

Mike nodded. That response made sense to him. "Well, have fun."

"We will," Phillip said. "Let's get to your house and the map," he whispered to Jackson.

The two of them raced next door and into Jackson's house. In seconds, they were in Jackson's room.

"Here's the book, Jackson." Phillip handed her the green book.

"The Yearly Census Book," Jackson read from the cover.

"Yeah, but everyone calls it the nosy book. We have thirty streets we need to look up," Phillip said. "Where's your list?"

"Over here, on my desk, I think."

Jackson shuffled around, tossing papers here and there.

"Shoot, I can't find it," Jackson said.

"Did you save it on your hard drive?"

"Yes! I'm glad that I decided to do it on the computer."

Jackson sat at her desk, and clicked her mouse three times. The printer gurgled and hummed, and came alive. Out churned the list of streets which Jackson had typed in earlier. She grabbed the page as the printer released it, and placed it on the floor next to the map.

"I'll read each street inside the circle on the map, and you can look them up in your book. If there's a Robert who lives within four-hundred yards of your house, we'll find him. Ready?" Jackson asked.

"Fine."

"Arlington Street," Jackson read to Phillip.

"Let me see," Phillip muttered as he flipped through the nosy book. He found Arlington Street. Below the street name was a list of everyone who lived on the street. He slowly moved his finger down through that list of names. He finally got to the bottom of the list and said, "No Bobs there."

"Are you looking for Robert? Bob is just a nickname," Jackson said.

"Oh yeah, I forgot. Let's see. One Robert. He's seventy-eight years old and he lives alone. Not it."

"Blue Ridge Drive," Jackson read from her list.

Phillip flipped pages until he found that street. "No. Only five houses on that street," he said.

"Waverley Avenue."

He turned to the end of the book.

"That's a long one. Give me a minute. Let's see...Two Roberts! One of them is age thirty-eight. Wife is Jennifer. They have two girls, ages seven and ten."

"That could be it!" Jackson screamed.

"No," Phillip said, "I forgot one other thing. There's a baby in the family."

"A baby?"

"Yeah."

"How old?" Jackson asked.

"I'm not sure. Somewhere between just born and probably four."

Jackson shook her head in amazement. "This is the strangest thing I ever heard of. It's lucky you're my best friend. No way would I do this for anyone else without knowing what's going on. What about the other Robert?"

"No. No kids."

"What's the next street?"

"Denton Drive," Jackson said.

Phillip moved his finger down the row of names. "One Robert on Denton, Robert Bailey. And this could be it! He's forty-two years old. Wife, Camille, age forty. Children, Gretchen, age nine, Kirsten, age six and Ross age two."

"But you said all the kids had to be girls," Jackson said.

"All the kids who aren't babies."

"Well, thanks for telling me now," Jackson groaned. "Are you sure you finally have it straight?"

Phillip tried to recall the conversation he had overheard. The parents were going to tell the girls about Annie going to Florida. They wouldn't have to tell the baby about Annie.

"Yeah. Sorry, Jackson. But write down this address. This family definitely fits the description."

Phillip and Jackson spent two hours going through each street within the four-hundred yard radius. At the end they had a list of five possible addresses, including Robert Bailey. Robert Harris on Granger Street had fours girls, ages three through thirteen. Robert Smith lived on Smith Street of all places, and he had two daughters, ages three and six. Robert Valentine on Cherry Hill Road had two daughters, ages eight and ten, and a

one year-old infant son. Finally, on Beal Street, was Robert
Hallman. He had three girls, ages two, four and seven. It was
probably one of those families. Phillip was almost certain that
there was a dead lady named Annie buried in a rose garden at
one of those five houses. He shuddered as he read the
addresses one more time.

CHAPTER 9

It had been a long night. Phillip's clock said five AM, and he was pretty sure that he would not be going back to sleep. Usually Emily's crying at night didn't bother him. He hardly heard it. His mother often complained about being up half the night with a screaming Emily, yet Phillip would have heard nothing. But tonight he had heard every sound from Emily's room. He heard each cough, cry and gurgle. It had been a very long night. Phillip just lay awake and listened. Crick...creak.... crick...creak. It was the squeak of the floorboards as the rocking chair in Emily's room moved back and forth. His mother had logged lots of mileage in that rocker these past months. He couldn't believe that his mother was up now. How much had she slept?

Phillip couldn't get the murder out of his mind. He had a Sunday game today at three, but he couldn't think about that at all. He had finally decided upon a course of action with his detective work. He would check out the five addresses and see if any had a rose garden. If just one did, then he had the address. If more than one had a rose garden, he'd have to listen to the parents talk, and see if any of the voices were familiar. He could also look at the rose garden and see if the dirt seemed recently dug up. Phillip had once read a mystery which was solved when a detective noticed fresh dirt on the ground. It was hard to be alone with these ideas bouncing around in his head. It would have been easier had he told Jackson, but it was better he hadn't. There was no need for the two of them to lose sleep over it all. Yet the urge to tell someone was almost too much. Instinctively, he got up and walked into Emily's room where his mother was still rocking the baby.

"Ugh!" Dara cried. "You scared me Phillip."

"Sorry, Mom. I just couldn't sleep."

"Join the club. God, it's been a rough night. I thought she was getting better, and then this. Three steps forward, one backward. That's the way it goes."

Phillip sat without saying a word, mesmerized by the rocking motion of his mother with Emily. Emily appeared to be asleep.

"What are you doing awake, Phillip?"

"Just thinking, Mom."

"About what?"

"It's kind of a long story."

"I'd love to hear it, Phillip, but I think that Emily is asleep now, and I have to get back to bed myself. I don't think I slept more than two hours last night."

"Why can't Mike help?"

"Mike's sweet. He does try to help, but he can't settle her at night. If I let him do it, she'd be awake all night and so would everyone else in the family. I can usually keep her quiet enough, and then at least you guys can sleep."

Phillip felt that he might tell her all about the monitor and the dead body right then, but just as he was ready to talk, Dara was up and placing Emily back in her crib.

"Good night, Phillip." Dara walked out, as if in a trance.

In the old days, Phillip would have told her everything. The old days. They had been just three months earlier, but they seemed like years ago. Phillip needed to tell someone. He couldn't keep it inside anymore. He wanted so much to share everything with his mother. But she was too tired. She was always too tired. Did she still love him? Phillip felt sad. Maybe he would have to tell Jackson.

Phillip tiptoed down the stairs and very quietly opened the front door and let himself out. It was still mostly dark, but a corner of the sky was starting to brighten. He felt funny walking in his pajamas and bare feet across his yard. He darted into Jackson's yard and stood below her window. Luckily she had a room of her own. He had done this a few times before, but always early at night, not at five in the morning. He grabbed some pebbles from the driveway and tossed one at Jackson's second floor window. It was a little low. It hit the side of the house. He tried throwing two the next time. One hit a window near Jackson's and one was high. Phillip wasn't sure if he hit Ben's window or Jackson's parents' window. Phillip ran behind a tree in the yard. A window opened. Phillip peaked out from behind the tree. It was Jackson, at *her* window!

"Jackson!" Phillip whispered loudly.

"I'll be right down," she whispered back.

In less than a minute, the back door opened. Jackson's eyes shone brightly as she let Phillip in. "Let's go down to the basement," she whispered, as she quietly closed the back door.

Phillip followed Jackson down the stairs into the basement family room. She jumped onto the soft leather sofa along the paneled wall. "We can talk down here. They won't be able to hear us."

Phillip plopped down in the bean bag chair on the floor. Jackson began to giggle. Then the giggle turned into a chuckle. In moments she was laughing hysterically. Phillip was puzzled.

"What's so funny?"

Jackson just pointed at Phillip. He looked down and breathed a sigh of relief. He wasn't flying low. That would be really embarrassing with his pajamas on and no underwear underneath. He was looking down at his pajamas and it suddenly hit him. He was wearing his cowboy pajamas! These were the ones that his father had given him for his birthday when he was six. Except his father never knew his size. They were huge. His mom had put them away for him to grow into. Five years later, he finally did grow into them. Hey, pajamas were pajamas. Who would see him in them?

"My Dad got them for me."

"I guess he really knows your taste," Jackson said, still grinning.

"Yeah," Phillip said with a laugh. Jackson was wearing a faded Mickey Mouse tee shirt which hung down below her knees. It was probably one of Ben's old shirts. She wore a lot of Ben's hand-me-downs. Phillip thought she looked good in Mickey Mouse. Jackson didn't dress at all like most other girls. She always said how dumb it was that they wasted so much time worrying about how they looked. "So, how did you know it was me? I missed your window with my pebble. I got the one next to yours. I was afraid it was your parents' room."

"It wasn't. It was Ben's room. He heard the pebble, and he assumed it was you. Who else would throw a pebble at one of our windows in the middle of the night? Besides, he's seen you play ball, and he knows what your aim is like," Jackson teased.

"I guess I was lucky I got him and not your parents."

"Just a little lucky. If you were going to hit a window near mine, you had a only fifty-fifty chance of hitting my parents' window. So, what did you want? A game of Mastermind?"

"I couldn't sleep."

"You wake me up in the middle of the night because you can't sleep?" she asked, giggling again.

"It's not the middle of the night. It's almost morning."

"No. I went to bed at midnight. I planned to sleep until ten in the morning. That makes it the middle of the night to me," Jackson said. "So, tell me, what's up?"

"I'm scared, Jackson."

"Scared? Really scared?" Jackson asked seriously.

"I'm not sure."

"What are you afraid of?"

"I'm afraid of the thing you're helping me with. I'm afraid of doing it alone, but I'm more afraid of telling you and making you not sleep at night either. I've dragged you in too much already."

"But Phillip, we've always been able to tell each other everything. You're the best friend that I've ever had. I've always told you everything. You can trust me."

"I know that I can trust you, Jackson. But this is really dangerous. Not kid dangerous, but serious, adult dangerous."

"I know this whole mystery thing is bothering you, but is there something else too?"

"Sort of."

"I sort of thought so. What else is it, Phillip?"

"It's my whole family. I'm not visiting my father this summer because he has a new job and he's too busy. All Mike wants to do is to turn me into a ball player I can never be. And my mom. I'm afraid my mom isn't going to have any more time for me anymore. You're my best friend, but she was my best friend too. She isn't anymore."

"Oh, Phillip," Jackson said, getting up and walking across the room. She sat back next to him on the beanbag chair and reached for his hand. She clasped his right hand in between both of hers, much like his mother used to do. She then let go and looked directly into his eyes. "It'll be all right. Your mom loves you. It'll turn out great in the end. It will be different when Emily gets just a little older. My mom told me that she thought that your mom was going through something called post-parthenon depression, or something like that."

"That sounds like something we studied in Ancient History. What is it?"

"She said that sometimes after a baby gets born, it's hard on a mother and she gets into a lot of bad moods. But it does get better. She told me not to say anything about it, that it's none of our business. But that's what it is. My mom said it won't be long before she's back to her old self."

Phillip was filled with hope.

"And you know," Jackson continued, "if you want to tell me about the other thing, that's fine. If you don't that's okay too."

Phillip shut his eyes and felt happy for a change. He lay back on the chair with Jackson sitting close to him. He wouldn't dream of sitting this close to a girl, but it was just Jackson, and it felt right. A guy couldn't have a better friend. Finally relaxed, he drifted off to sleep.

The sun was shining into his face through the basement window high above the couch. He looked at the clock over the TV. Nine o'clock! He had been asleep for three hours! Jackson lay sound asleep next to him on the bean bag chair. Phillip shook her awake.

"We've been sleeping for three hours!"

"Really," she said, slowly opening her eyes. "What time is it?"

"Nine. What if my parents checked my room? They'll wonder where I am! I have to get back to my house."

Phillip jumped up and began to run up the stairs.

"Wait," Jackson called. "You're going to walk outside like that?" She pointed to his cowboy pajamas. "And what will your parents say when you stroll in through the front door?"

"What should I do?"

"Let me think." She paused. "I have it! You can put on one of Ben's bathing suits. If your parents see you, tell them that you saw me running in the sprinkler early in the morning. My parents usually turn it on then to water the lawn. And that you borrowed one of Ben's suits so you wouldn't wake anyone up by going back in to get your own."

What a good idea. How does Jackson think of things like that so quickly?

"Great!" Phillip said.

Jackson ran upstairs and came down with one of Ben's suits, a red one. She had even wet it first. Jackson walked up stairs and waited while he put in on. Then he started up the stairs himself as he called to her, "What if your parents see me?"

"Don't worry about them. I'll just tell them the truth."

"They won't be mad?" Phillip asked.

"No."

"Then why 'd you say that I was lucky that I didn't hit their window?"

"They wouldn't mind you over here, but they'd be ticked off at being woken up at five in the morning!"

Phillip smiled. "Gotta run. Thanks for everything."

CHAPTER 10

Phillip slipped into his house and tip-toed up to his room unnoticed. No need for the excuse Jackson had come up with. It was a great one anyway. Phillip spotted his uniform on top of his dresser. His mother had just washed it for today's game. But the game was not really on his mind. He knew that he would have to deal with the 'Bob' thing now. One way or another, it would be resolved today.

He took off Ben's bathing suit and got dressed into his regular clothes. Next, Phillip walked to his desk and grabbed the bag which he had put together with Jackson. It had the street map and the addresses of the five possible Bobs. He was now glad that he had decided to do it alone and not drag Jackson into it. Phillip looked once more into the bag and made sure all the stuff was there, then he folded up the top, and walked downstairs. No one was around. Where were they? Did they wonder where he was, and were they looking for him? Did they call the police? Suddenly, Phillip was very concerned.

He stepped into the living room. The baby monitor was on, as it usually was, even when Emily was not asleep. Phillip couldn't help himself. He turned the frequency to 8.4. Nothing. He was adjusting the frequency the tiniest amount when a door slammed and Phillip jumped a mile!

Dara entered the living room with a laundry basket filled with just dried clothes.

"At last, our almost teenager is up."

"What was that slam, Mom?"

"Just the door to the cellar. The wind did it. Were you scared?"

"Oh, no," Phillip said. "Where's Mike and Emily?"

"Mike's walking her in the stroller, giving me a chance to get some chores done around here. What are you doing with the monitor?"

"Oh, nothing. Just messing around. Actually, I was wondering if you guys were upstairs with Emily, and I was turning up the volume."

Dara looked at Phillip as if she did not believe him. "Just make sure that you leave the monitor as it was when you found it. Yesterday the frequency was changed and I didn't hear Emily call for a long time. I have no idea how long she was wailing for."

"I will, Mom. Sorry about yesterday."

"That's okay. I was napping on the couch. I did get a little extra nap time which I needed. Maybe I should thank you."

Phillip smiled. "Oh, and Mom, I'm going outside."

"Where are you going?"

"Uh..."

"And what's in that bag?"

"Oh, just a, uh, a...uh, a map. I'm exploring some of the other streets in the neighborhood. Jackson lent me this map and I thought that it would be fun to explore with it."

"That sounds like fun. Be careful."

"Bye, Mom."

"Wait." Dara looked serious and paused. Phillip got nervous.

"Phillip, did you have breakfast yet?"

"No. I'll do it now, then go out."

"Great."

Phillip grabbed a glass of juice and made a quick bowl of cereal. Within five minutes, he was out the door. Robert Bailey first. Phillip checked out the directions to Denton Drive. He was pretty sure he knew where Denton was anyway. He decided that he would walk instead of ride his bike. It would be a pain to carry the bag on a bike. It took him about ten minutes to walk to Denton. Next step, look for number 55. The first house he saw was on the left, and it was number 79. That meant that the Bailey house was on the left. All the odd numbered houses are on one side of a street and the even ones are on the other. Phillip quickly determined that the numbers were going down, and so he was close. A minute later he was there. He looked up at the possible scene of the crime—a red brick house with black shutters. It looked like a regular house, not a house where murderers live. But what did he expect? No one seemed to be around. He went to the driveway and tried to peer into the back yard. There was some kind of a garden back there, but he couldn't tell if there were roses. Should he go back and check? He was scared. What if they were home? What if they asked what he was doing back there? Jackson would certainly think of a great excuse. She was good at that. Phillip had to use his head. He had to be ready in case. It really might be a matter of life or death. Phillip paused. What was he doing, he asked himself. He was just a kid! He shouldn't be doing this, but what else could he do? Once he knew who the real Bob was, then he could call the police, but not now. They'd never believe a kid without more information, information they could check out themselves. And if Phillip didn't act soon, then these guys might murder again. He had to try to stop that from happening.

Phillip racked his brain for an excuse if he got caught. Why would a kid be in a stranger's back yard? Phillip thought and thought. Looking for a baseball! No, that doesn't make sense. Why would his baseball be lost in this guy's yard? A dog! That's it! He'd be looking for his dog. He thought he saw it go in their yard. That's the kind of excuse Jackson would come up with. He couldn't wait to tell her. She'd be proud of him.

Phillip ran into the backyard. There were tomatoes growing, and some other vegetables and even flowers. But no roses. One down, four to go.

In the next hour, Phillip tracked down three more Roberts. There was no one around in any of the houses. Armed with an excellent excuse, Phillip didn't give it a thought when he barged onto each property searching for a rose garden. No roses in any of them. The last place left to check was on Beal Street. Robert Hallman. But what if this wasn't the one? What would he do then? Phillip decided to worry about that if and when that happened. This had to be the right one. Unless someone new moved to town. Oh, no. Don't worry about that now, Phillip told himself. It took a while to get to Beal. It was almost one o'clock now. His game was in two hours.

Phillip tracked down number 324 Beal. Beal was a main street, and so at least Phillip didn't attract attention walking on the side walk. 324 Beal was a huge white house with a porch in front and a big front lawn. And there was a man mowing the lawn! Oh no! What should he do? A chill crept up his spine. He was afraid. This was probably the guy. The man had black hair and bushy dark eyebrows. But he didn't look like a killer. Phillip stopped at the driveway and tried to look into the back yard. A woman was weeding a garden along the side of the house. She saw Phillip looking her way.

"Can I help you?" Her voice sounded a little like the one on the monitor. It was hard to tell, though, without all the static.

Phillip breathed deeply and walked up the driveway towards her. He heard girls' voices in the back yard. "Excuse me," Phillip said. His voice was quivering. He didn't want to sound nervous but he couldn't help himself. "Excuse me, but I lost my dog, and I thought that I saw him go this way."

"What kind of dog was it?" the woman asked.

He wasn't ready for that question! "Uh," he hesitated, "a Dalmatian." That was the kind of dog Jackson had.

"Oh, no. I would have noticed an unusual dog like that. No Dalmatian here."

What a stupid kind of dog to come up with! Kids don't have Dalmatians.

"Can I please take a look back there?" Phillip asked nervously.

"You sound pretty upset. I know what it's like to lose a pet. It happened with us not too long ago. Sure, you can look if it will make you feel better."

"Thank you," Phillip said. She seemed so nice. She couldn't possibly be a murderer.

Phillip walked into the back yard. The two older girls, the ones the nosy book said were seven and four years old, were on swings, while the two year-old was picking at flowers in the garden.

The mother called back, "Keep Julia out of the garden! I don't want her pulling up the flowers, or pricking herself on the thorns."

"Yes, Mom," the oldest daughter answered.

Thorns! Thorns meant roses! This must be it! These *must* be the murderers! Phillip grew courageous and stepped closer to the garden. Then he saw it. There was one spot which clearly had been recently dug up. The area was about four feet long and two feet wide. Big enough if you fold over a body. This was the right place.

The older girl walked up to the baby and dragged her from the garden. She smiled at Phillip. A pang of sadness struck him. How their lives will change when they find out their parents are killers, when their mom and dad go to jail. The kids seemed like nice girls. The parents might be good parents, but they were killers too.

Without saying a word, Phillip ran down the driveway.

"Did you find it?" the mother's voice trailed away as he ran.

Phillip didn't answer. He was too excited. And scared.

CHAPTER 11

"I was worried that you forgot about your game, Phillip,"
Dara said.

Phillip was surprised that she even remembered about his
game. Not that it made a big difference if he forgot about it. The
team wouldn't miss him. Coach Higgins would be thrilled not to
have to stick him in for his two innings. Even Phillip would
rather not play today. There were more important things on his
mind. But Phillip did have a certain sense of responsibility.
Baseball was sort of like school. You showed up because you
were supposed to.

"Your uniform is up in your room, on top of your bureau."

"I know."

"Did you have lunch?"

"No, but I'm not very hungry, Mom."

"Phillip, you have a baseball game. You need a good lunch to
be ready for that."

"For what, to warm the bench? The most I'll do is play right
field for an inning or two and maybe get up once. I can do that
on an empty stomach."

"You don't sound too happy about playing. Don't you enjoy
baseball this season?" Dara asked with concern.

Where have you been, Mom, Phillip thought. He just shrugged
his shoulders.

"Do you want to quit?"

"No way," Phillip said instinctively. On second thought, why didn't he want to quit? He didn't particularly enjoy the games. But Phillip wasn't a quitter. When he started something, he finished it. But it was more than that. Even though he stunk, he still loved the game of baseball. He loved watching it, and trying to play it. Just being part of a team, even the bench-warmer, was fun. And the other guys on the team weren't too bad. At school, most of the kids either made fun of him or they just ignored him. They thought that he was too smart. The same thing used to happen to his real dad when he was a kid. But on the baseball team, it wasn't as bad as at school.

Some of the guys teased him, but he was used to that. And just the most serious players, especially Art, hated him because he was lousy. But a lot of the other kids seemed to like him. Maybe it was that they were impressed with how much he knew about baseball. They were always asking him questions about the rules of the game or about major leaguers or baseball history. Or maybe it was that the other players didn't like Coach Higgins very much, and they felt protective when he picked on Phillip. Whatever the reason, Phillip mostly did like being part of the team.

"Well, I'll feel better watching you play if you have a little to eat, so do it for me, will you?"

"You're coming today?" Phillip asked excitedly.

"Yeah. It's a good time for Emily. She'll just be finished her nap and it's before that bewitching dinner hour. She likes to be outside, and so she probably won't drive everyone crazy there. So go get in your uniform while I make you a sandwich."

"Okay," Philip said as he turned around and headed upstairs.

"Peanut butter and jelly?" Dara whispered loudly.

"Yup," Phillip whispered back without turning around at the top of the stairs.

In less than five minutes Phillip was downstairs in the kitchen with his peanut butter sandwich and a glass of milk in front of him.

"Is Mike coming?" Phillip asked his mother.

"Not today. He has his own softball game."

Phillip was even happier. He tried to hide his smile, but couldn't conceal it completely.

"Now Phillip, Mike really does care about you and your baseball. He loves going to your games. Not all the other parents go as much as he does."

"Yeah, I know, Mom. But I always feel worse when I screw up and he's watching. I feel like I'm letting him down."

"He only wants what's best for you, Phillip. He does love you."

"I think he wants what's best for him. He wants a star player he can be proud of and brag about to the guys at work and the guys on his softball team, guys like Walter."

Dara grimaced at the mention of Walter. "That really isn't true. He is pretty competitive, and it looks that way sometimes, but it isn't true. I wish that you would let him work on your game with you. He would love to do that. It would be a good thing for you guys to share together."

"It wouldn't do any good, Mom. I stink and I won't get any better. It's in the genes. I have Dad's sports genes. He always said how bad he was at sports. The only sports team he ever played on was an ultimate Frisbee team in college. They didn't even play other schools, and the only people on the teams were math and science guys."

"There are math and science guys who are good athletes. Look at Mr. Curcio. He used to be a star basketball player, and now he coaches the high school varsity team. And you know how smart he is at math."

She did have a point. "There are exceptions to every rule."

"Then you might be one. There are good sports genes in my family."

"But Mom, you throw a baseball like a girl."

"That's only because I never played the game when I was young. And not all girls 'throw like girls.'"

"I know that. Maggie on our team is awesome."

"It's just that most girls don't spend half their younger life throwing balls and developing a 'boy throw.' Anyway, I was the star of my high school soccer team. It was the first girl's soccer team in our school. I was one of the ones who pushed to make it happen, and I was pretty good. I ran track, too, and was a very good sprinter."

"Was there always a boys soccer team?"

"Yes."

"And no girls team? I thought that they can't do that."

"Things were different twenty-five years ago. There were almost no girl's teams then. Girls weren't expected to play sports."

"That's pretty funny," Phillip said. "So what did they do instead?"

Dara stopped and thought for a moment. "You know, I can't remember. Anyway, Phillip, you need to eat and get to the game. I'd better get out so you can stop talking and eat. I have a few things to do in the yard. I'll be right back in. Now, eat!"

"Yes, Mom," Phillip said, taking a second bite of his sandwich.

Phillip was actually excited about the game with his mom going and Mike not going. He was so focused on the game that he actually forgot about Robert Hallman on Beal Street for a few minutes. But Robert couldn't stay out of his mind for long. After the game, Phillip would call the police. Then his part would be done. The police would do the rest.

Phillip grabbed his baseball glove from the back hall closet, and passed his mother as she was coming in while he was going out.

"I'll be there for the start of the game. I'll wake Emily if I have to, and I can feed her at the game."

"Mom, you're not going to breast feed her at the game! Not in front of all the guys and their parents!" Dara was pretty casual about when and where she would nurse the baby.

"I'll stay way out in left field for that, Phillip. No one will notice, I promise."

"Okay, Mom. See you soon." Phillip ran off to the pre-game practice.

"Phillip, do you have a signed shirt from Cards and Comics?" Lars asked.

"I didn't even hear about them. What kind of shirts?"

"Baseball shirts, signed by All-Stars in both leagues. There's a special. Fifty bucks apiece, mostly. A little more for guys like Sammy Sosa or Mark McGwire."

"Wow, what a deal!" Phillip said. "How can they sell them at that price?"

"They deal in volume. That's why they call it a superstore."

Still, a pretty incredible price.

"And my dad bought a Sandy Koufax rookie card there for $400," Harry said. "Card Digest says it's worth $1400 in mint condition. And this card was perfect, like it's never been touched."

"I don't understand..." Phillip began.

"Phillip, you're up next. Get a bat and swing," Coach Higgins interrupted.

Phillip jumped from the bench and grabbed a bat. He slid the red donut over the knob of the bat and grabbed a helmet, then headed to the on-deck circle. He was psyched that the Braves had a six run lead. Otherwise he never would be in the line-up in the fourth inning, particularly when it means getting up before he plays the field. That means that he might even hit twice this game! Maggie Dwyer was up now. The Braves were playing the Jack's Joke Shop Pirates. What a name for a team. Jack's Joke Shop was a neat store. It was filled with some pretty funny things. Phillip had bought Mike a couple of presents there. One was a plastic guy, and when you pulled down his pants, he peed at you. Not real pee, just water. Mike had loved it. It was a great store, but Phillip wouldn't want his baseball team to have the word 'joke' in it. Whenever Jack's Joke Shop lost, the other team usually made cracks like, 'You guys are a joke.' Usually they weren't a joke. Billy Harris was their regular pitcher, and he threw the ball faster than anyone in the league. He usually won, but today his control was pretty bad. It was the top of the fourth and the Pizza House Braves were up 6-0. Five of the runs had been scored when Billy walked just about everyone in the lineup in the second inning. A walk to Art and a double by Lars in the third had given the Braves their last run.

The count was 3-and-1 on Maggie. Billy wound up and threw a fastball for a call strike. Coach Higgins had given Maggie the red light. With Billy's speed, he was hoping for a walk. But with a 3-2 count now, Maggie would have to hit away. Sure enough, Coach rubbed his left elbow. Green light. The pitch came in. High and outside. Maggie held back her swing. Ball four.

Phillip popped the donut off his bat and tossed it into the on-deck circle. He then stepped up to the plate. He looked into the stands and spotted his mother holding Emily. And next to her was Mike! He must have finished his own game. Why couldn't he have gone out for a few beers afterwards with the guys? Phillip didn't want Mike to watch while he batted against Billy Harris.

Phillip looked to Coach Higgins. He rubbed his right wrist and tipped his cap. Red light. Billy Harris wound up and fired. Right over the plate, strike one. And fast! Phillip shuddered at the speed of the ball. He had never seen such a fast pitch! What if it hit him? The thought terrified Phillip. He took a step back away from the plate.

"Get back in there, Phillip. Closer to the plate!" Coach Higgins ordered.

Phillip inched a little closer. He looked at his coach. The left elbow. Green light. Coach Higgins wanted him to swing if it was over the plate. Billy glared at Phillip, trying to scare him. It worked. Billy wound up and threw.

"Ball one," the umpire called. It went so fast that Phillip hardly even saw it. He wouldn't have swung at it even if it had been over. Next time, he would really be ready. He needed to be against this guy.

Phillip looked towards his coach again. Green light. Billy pitched. Phillip stood frozen as it went by his eyes. A little inside. It almost hit him! The count was 2-and-1. Coach Higgins gave Phillip the red light. The next pitch was outside for a ball. Maybe he'd get a walk! The count was 3-and-1. Phillip expected the red light now. Even Maggie had been given the red light with a 3-and-1 count against Billy Harris. There was little chance Billy would put two in a row over the plate. Coach Higgins gave Phillip the red light. Billy Harris let up, and threw a slow one over the plate for a strike. I could have hit that one, Phillip thought. If the next one is that slow, I'll nail it!

There was a 3-and-2 count now. Phillip was excited and confident. He wasn't afraid. He'd show Mike and Coach Higgins what he could do here. Phillip was sure that Billy Harris had lost confidence in his fastball. He's coming with another easy change-up. Phillip glanced at his coach. Coach Higgins rubbed his right wrist and tipped his cap. It can't be! He can't give me the red light with a full count! That's wrong anytime. You have to let a guy swing if it's good, especially when their fastballer has lost his nerve and is serving up gopher balls. Phillip looked at his coach and shook his head no. He must be giving the wrong signal accidentally. Phillip backed out of the batting box and looked again down to third. Coach Higgins repeated the red light signal. Phillip knew it was wrong, but it was also a player's job to follow the instructions of his coach. What should he do? Once John McGraw told a player to bunt. The hitter had disobeyed his coach and swung away, and hit a game winning home run. McGraw had fined the guy. That was about sixty years ago. Phillip wasn't sure what he would do now. He stepped into the batting box and looked at Billy Harris. Billy's scary stare was gone. He even looked a little nervous. Finally, he wound up and pitched. Phillip followed his coach's instructions and did not swing. A slow ball sailed right over the heart of the plate. Strike three.

Phillip trudged back to the bench. He looked towards the stands and spotted his mother and Mike. His mom wore a forced smile on her face but was clapping anyway as if to say 'Nice try.' Mike was shaking his head in disgust. It wasn't my fault, Phillip wanted to tell them. The coach told me not to swing. But he couldn't tell them. He didn't blame Mike for being disgusted. He should be disgusted at a guy for letting a 3-and-2 meatball go down the pike without swinging at it.

"Hey, saber man, why didn't you swing?" Jack asked.

"He's a loser," Art said in disgust.

"Maybe you should just keep stats," Gary said.

"Coach Higgins gave me the red light," Phillip said meekly.

"Get outta here," Art said. "You don't give anyone the red light on a full count. You just wish he did that. Then you wouldn't have to swing and miss the ball. Beside, it's easier to duck if you don't swing."

The other kids laughed and turned back towards the game. Lars came over to Phillip and sat down next to him.

"Did he really give you the red light?" Lars asked.

"He did, I swear it."

"I believe you, Phillip. Higgins is a loser. It's not your fault."

"Thanks, Lars."

"The other kids know he's a loser. I heard that he used to play minor league ball, and the only reason he coaches us is because he wasn't good enough as a player and he wants to make up for it with us. He's the only coach in the league who doesn't have a kid on his team. My dad said he's just a frustrated ex-player. So don't worry about him."

The inning soon ended, and Phillip ran out to right field. One ball came his way. It was a fly ball that went over his head. Phillip ran back to the fence, picked up the ball, and threw a pretty good relay to the cut-off at second. The Pirates got three runs that half inning, and so Coach Higgins took Phillip out after his two innings. He didn't get another chance to bat.

Phillip just sat glumly on the bench. He began to think about what he had to do afterwards. He wasn't sure what was depressing him more, the Robert Hallman thing, or this game. Both were pretty unpleasant.

The Braves did hold on to win the game, 7-5. Coach Higgins was happy. He hadn't expected to beat the Jack's Joke Shop Pirates, not with Billy Harris on the mound today. But the Braves did win, and everyone was going crazy. Everyone except Phillip.

His mother and Mike came up to Phillip after the handshake. "Nice game," Dara said. Mike said nothing. It wasn't even worth telling Mike that Higgins gave him the red light on the 3-2 pitch. Mike wouldn't believe him anyway, just like Art and the other guys didn't.

"I'll see you at home," Phillip mumbled, and ran ahead to make a very important phone call.

CHAPTER 12

Phillip's heart pounded as he ran in the front door. He only had a few minutes before his mom and Mike came home. It might be longer if they got talking to people, Phillip thought. He had to do it now. He decided to call from the upstairs phone in his parents' room so if they came in, he'd have more time and privacy.

He walked upstairs and sat on his parents' huge queen-size bed. The phone on the bedside table was a push-button with memory dial. The police was an emergency number programmed into memory. It was a button that his parents had made sure he knew. He pressed the blue button.

"Police emergency, Detective Stokes speaking. This call is being recorded."

Phillip's heart beat harder than ever.

"Hello. Uh, I'd like to report a murder. Are you the person I talk to?"

"Yes I am. Is this a joke, son?"

"N-No," Phillip stuttered. "I wish it were." He paused and then spit out quickly, "There's a dead body buried in a rose garden at 324 Beal Street. Robert Hallman is one of the people who did it. I think that his wife was involved, too."

"You're serious? It's a criminal act to falsely report a crime."

Phillip breathed deeply and then spoke into the phone more slowly, "Yes, I'm serious."

"What's your name, and the number that you're calling from?"

"Do I need to tell you?" Phillip asked hesitantly.

"Yes, you do, son."

Phillip breathed deeply. There was no turning back now. "Phillip Crafts."

"Phone number you're calling from?"

"688-8901."

"Is that your home phone, son?"

"Yes it is."

"Address?"

"62 Langworthy Road. Across from Andrews Field."

"Tell me what you know," Detective Stokes said calmly.

Phillip started to feel more relaxed. "You know those baby monitors?" he asked.

"Yes, I do."

"Well, my parents have a new baby, and I was listening to different frequencies. I was listening to other people's conversations, and heard one about burying someone called Annie in the back yard by the rose bushes. The father, Bob, was talking to his wife about what they would say to the kids. They decided to tell them that Annie had gone to live in Florida. Maybe Annie is their grandmother and they got sick of taking care of her or something. Anyway, that's what I heard."

"How did you find out the address?"

Phillip explained how he and his friend Jackson had used the nosy book to zero in on five possibilities, and how he had found a rose garden at only one of the addresses. He told about seeing the newly dug dirt in the garden. He made sure to say that Jackson knew nothing about the murder. She was only helping him out, and he wanted her to be kept out of it.

"Phillip, we're going to need to come over and take a formal statement," the detective said kindly.

"Please, don't! My parents don't know and I don't want to worry them. Isn't this enough?"

"Phillip, this is a very serious matter. Your parents will need to be involved. And I need to verify that you are who you say you are. We cannot very well barge into someone's yard and dig up a rose garden and then find out that this was a prank call. I do believe you, Phillip. But this statement is an essential formality."

Deep down, Phillip knew that the policeman was right. "Okay, I'm here. Are you coming now?"

"Yes. Are your parents home?"

"They're walking home from across the street at the park. They should be here any minute."

"Then we'll send some officers over right now."

"Will *you* come over?"

"I'm on desk detail now. I'll send two others."

"Please, can you come? I'm not nervous talking to you now. It would be a lot easier if you could come and talk to me."

"Just a minute, Phillip." The phone was put on hold, except there was no music in the background like there usually was on hold. "Phillip?" Detective Stokes was back.

"Yes?"

"I'll be there."

"Thanks."

"Be there soon. Sit tight. Everything's going to be all right. You've done the right thing."

Phillip hung up. He wasn't so nervous now. The hard part was over. He went down the stairs just as his mother and Mike were coming in with Emily. Emily was asleep in her mother's arms.

"Mom, Mike, there's something important that I have to tell you. Maybe you should sit down." In movies, adults always tell people to sit when they're breaking bad news. Mike and Dara nervously obeyed.

"Yes, Phillip?" Dara asked.

"The police are coming over now."

"The police!" Mike blurted.

"Why, Phillip?" Dara asked. "What's wrong? Are you in trouble?"

"Oh, no, Mom. But I just called them with information about a murder. They're on their way to take a formal statement from me. They wanted you guys here, too, so don't go anywhere."

"Trust me, we're not going anywhere," Dara said. "Who got murdered, and how did you get involved?"

"It's a long story, Mom. I just told Detective Stokes about it on the phone. I'll tell it again in a few minutes. I can't go all into it another time. Can you wait, please?"

"Oh, Phillip," Dara said as she handed over the sleeping Emily to Mike and rushed to hug her son.

"Mom, it's okay."

There was a knock on the front screen door.

"Mr. and Mrs. Crafts?"

Mike walked up and opened the door. "No, O'Hara. Mr. and Mrs. O'Hara. My step-son is Crafts, Phillip Crafts."

"My name is Tim Stokes, Detective Tim Stokes." Detective Stokes was about fifty years old and a big man. He looked sort of like Mr. Sweeny the umpire. Except Detective Stokes seemed much nicer.

"And I'm Officer Hardwick," his partner said. She was much smaller and younger and looked very business-like.

"Mike O'Hara. My wife, Dara." He pointed to Dara with one hand while holding Emily with the other. "And that's Phillip."

"Mr. and Mrs. O'Hara, your son did the right thing when he called us. Do you know any of what has happened?"

"Nothing," Dara said. "And I can't wait another minute to find out what's going on. Will someone tell me?"

"Phillip heard a conversation on your baby monitor from another family. There was talk of burying a woman in the back yard."

"Oh, God," Dara cried.

"It's all right, Mrs. O'Hara," Officer Hardwick said in a sooth-
ing tone. "We're going to take a formal statement now. I will
record it. We're just going to ask Phillip to tell us everything he
told us on the phone. If he remembers anything else, he should
say that too. That's all."

"Please sit down," Dara said as she got up and pulled chairs
from across the room and brought them closer to Phillip. Officer
Hardwick turned on her cassette recorder while Detective
Stokes asked Phillip to tell everything he knew.

It took about a half an hour for them to slowly go through
each detail. The police officers spent a lot of time questioning
Phillip, especially on exactly what he had heard over the monitor. At the end, Detective Hardwick asked, "Jackson lives next
door that way?"

"Yes, but please don't bring her into this. Please don't. I told
you, she knows nothing."

"I believe you, Phillip, but we have to talk to her. A murder is
a pretty serious crime, and we must touch every base,"
Detective Stokes said. He then nodded to Officer Hardwick, and
she went out the door.

About ten minutes later, Officer Hardwick showed up with
Jackson and her parents. She had probably been doing a lot of
explaining to her parents first.

"Hi, Jackson," Phillip said.

"Hi, Phillip."

"I want only Jackson to talk now. Phillip, do you think you
can stay in here and not say anything?"

Phillip nodded.

Dara tried to get everyone seated but Mr. and Mrs. Curcio
remained standing by the door.

"Jackson," Officer Hardwick said, "please tell us everything
that happened in regards to Mr. Robert Hallman."

Jackson told them everything. Everything, that is, except
about Phillip visiting her at five in the morning in his pajamas.

"Is that correct, Phillip?" Officer Hardwick asked.

"Yes, that's it."

"Are you going over there?" Phillip asked.

"No, there are two other officers ready to go now. They're waiting for our okay. Carol, tell them to move," Detective Stokes said to Officer Hardwick. She walked out to the police car parked in the street.

"That's all," Detective Stokes said. "Just stay away from the Hallman place. It's our job now. You did well, Phillip."

"When will we find out what happened?" Phillip asked.

"I can't say. Depends how things go. There's a confidentiality issue. If it all gets resolved through the courts or an arrest is made, then that is public record. I can tell you that. I have to see how it goes. I'll be in touch."

Detective Stokes left.

CHAPTER 13

"It's hard to believe that we were here just over twelve hours ago, and I didn't know anything that was going on," Jackson said, lying on the bean bag chair on the floor of the basement family room."

"Yeah," Phillip said from the couch. "Your parents were really cool about it. I was pretty scared when they were dragged in."

"I wasn't worried about my parents. Besides, you did the right thing. And I think that those police were pretty impressed by our detective work. As she left, Officer Hardwick gave me a nod and a little thumbs up. She was cool."

"I liked them both. I thought it would be a lot scarier than it was. Now that's it's over, it was kind of fun."

"It would have been more fun for me if I had known what was going on. But I understand why you didn't want to tell me. I still wish that you had. So, tell me more about Robert Hallman and his wife." Jackson's eyes glistened.

"Nothing special. Actually, they seemed like nice people with good kids. You'd never guess that they were killers."

"You never know, though," Jackson said, smiling. "Were you scared?"

"Yes. I was terrified!"

Jackson laughed and Phillip did too. It's a lot easier to laugh when something like this is over.

78

"Jackson, Phillip, come upstairs," Mrs. Curcio called from the kitchen upstairs. There was urgency in her voice.

Jackson and Phillip looked at each other. Puzzled, they hopped up and raced upstairs.

"What is it, Mom?" Jackson asked.

"The police just called your house, Phillip. They're heading over and want to talk to you."

Oh no, Phillip thought. Something went wrong.

"What about me?" Jackson asked.

"No, they said just Phillip. You'd better go home now, Phillip."

Phillip was scared. Jackson touched him on the shoulder and said, "Good luck. You did everything right. There's nothing to worry about."

"Thanks, Jackson."

Phillip left.

Mike, Dara and Emily were standing to greet him at his home when he arrived. They didn't say anything. Phillip walked in and headed to the living room. It seemed to be the interrogation room of choice in his house. They all sat down and waited. A long five minutes later, the police arrived. Detective Stokes was there. But instead of Officer Hardwick, another police officer was with him.

They knocked and entered.

"I'm Cable. I'm the detective who just investigated the Hallman place. I thought I'd inform you of what happened." Phillip didn't know if Cable was his first or last name.

Detective Stokes said nothing but had a sad look on his face. Cable was definitely angry. Phillip was scared. He sat close to his mother, and Dara put her arm around him.

"I assume you're Phillip," Cable said sharply.

"Yes."

"Well, your wild story caused quite a bit of unnecessary upset to a good family. It was terrible what they had to go through just because of you."

"What do you mean?" Mike asked. Phillip was relieved that Mike had spoken up. The words would not come out of Phillip's mouth.

"What do I mean! You accuse two good solid citizens of murder and you ask what I mean?" Cable exploded. "Do you know how embarrassing it is to barge in there, toss around accusations, and even try to dig up a body when no one's been murdered?"

Phillip dug down and found the courage to ask, "What about Annie?"

"Annie was their damn cat! The damn cat died, and they didn't want to break the hearts of their kids. So they buried their pet in their rose garden and told the kids that she had gone to Florida!"

Oh God, Phillip thought. It all made sense. How could this happen? Phillip looked at Detective Stokes, who gave him a sad but sympathetic smile. But he said nothing. Cable probably outranked him. And, come to think of it, Detective Stokes must be embarrassed and might even be in trouble himself. Phillip felt bad for him and Officer Hardwick.

"Have you been in trouble with the police before?" Cable asked.

"No," Phillip said, shaking his head.

"You look familiar." Cable looked at Phillip carefully and paused. "Wait, you're the baseball kid! Right?"

"Huh?"

"You're the kid who sawed the goddamn bat against the Pharmacy Phillies, aren't you?"

Phillip nodded.

"Well, I'll be a...Kid, you're a loony toon. My kid's on the Pharmacy. I was at that game. It's one thing to make up crazy baseball plots and saw a bat in two. It's another to accuse real people of murder. Wake up to reality. You're a dangerous kid."

Dara looked at Phillip as if to ask what's going on. She didn't know about the sawed bat, but she said nothing.

"And what you did with that monitor was wrong. You have no right to listen into other people's houses. What about respect for their privacy? How would you like if some snot-nosed kid listened to everything in your house?"

Phillip hung his head in shame. He knew that Cable was right about that.

"Kid, if you like mysteries, stick to reading them and stay out of real people's lives." Cable then turned to Detective Stokes and said, "Let's go."

As the policemen left, Cable gave Phillip one last nasty glare while Detective Stokes nodded kindly to him.

"Mr. and Mrs. O'Hara, keep your eye on that kid of yours," Cable said from outside the doorway. The police left.

Dara turned to Phillip and said, "I think you have more explaining to do."

"Not now, Mom, please?" Phillip begged.

"What's this about the sawed off bat? It sounds like a pretty big thing! How can you not tell me? And you hear about a murder and don't even mention it to me? Phillip, you used to tell me everything in your life!"

"It's not my fault. It's you who's always too busy or tired or in a bad mood. I've tried talking so much and you haven't been there. You're there for Emily but not for me."

"Oh, Phillip! Let's talk now," Dara pleaded, trying to hide the hurt look on her face.

"Later," Phillip said and stomped out of the living room. He ran up to his room, slammed the door shut, lay down on his bed and cried.

Chapter 14

"Phillip, come on down for dinner," Dara called as if nothing had happened.

Phillip just lay on his bed, staring mindlessly at Tony LaRussa on the ceiling. Tony absolutely would never have done anything this stupid. Phillip felt overwhelmed with embarrassment. He didn't want to face his parents. He didn't want to face the kids at school or the kids on his team. Word would certainly get out, and this would be worse than the sawed bat thing. Phillip didn't even want to face Jackson. He'd have to do it, though. He owed it to her.

"Phillip, come on down to dinner." This time Dara's voice was coming from right outside his room.

Phillip ignored her.

"Phillip?"

"Stay away please."

"But Phillip, dinner is ready."

"I'm not hungry."

"Can I come in?"

"No," Phillip said quietly.

"Please talk to me," Dara said, knocking on the door and opening it at the same time. Dara was holding Emily, who had a big grin on her face.

"Even Emily thinks I'm a fool."

"You're not a fool, Phillip. It was an honest mistake. You did the right thing. Even Detective Stokes said so."

"He didn't say that the last time he came over. He didn't say a word, then."

"But he didn't say you were stupid, either. He's probably taking a lot of heat over this himself."

True, Phillip thought.

"Phillip, I mean this. If I had ever heard what you heard, and I knew the people's address, I would have called the police just like you did. It was bad luck that what you heard could so easily be misinterpreted. Don't feel bad."

"I don't think that the other guys will look at it that way."

"Who cares what the other guys think?"

"I do. It's not fun being laughed at, Mom."

"I know. But they'll forget about it. They will. Why don't you come and eat?"

"I don't feel like it. But if it's all right, can I go over to Jackson's? I should tell her all about it."

"Sure."

"Thanks, Mom."

Phillip walked down stairs, past Mike, and out the door. In a minute, he was at the Curcio back door. He knocked, and walked in.

"It's the ace detective," Jackson said from the dinner table when she saw Phillip.

"Phillip, you're awesome," Ben said, his eyes filled with admiration.

"Phillip, what you did was truly impressive," Mr. Curcio added.

"Let me get a place for you to eat," Mrs. Curcio said, getting up. "Is everything okay?"

"I'm not hungry, thank you anyway," Phillip said. "I just came over to say something to Jackson, but I guess I should tell you all."

"What is it, Phillip?" asked Mrs. Curcio. Her tone of voice indicated that she knew that there was something wrong.

"It's bad. Actually, it's good, I guess. No one was murdered."

"What about Annie?" Jackson asked.

"Annie was their cat."

Silence. No one knew what to say.

"Pretty dumb, huh? I guess I'm not as smart as I thought. I'm just a stupid kid. I never should have acted like I was a real detective. I guess I've read too many Hardy Boy books."

"Phillip, you did the right thing," Mr. Curcio said. "I think that you know you did. It was just a tough break. But it is good that no one was really killed."

"I guess," Phillip said glumly.

"Phillip, despite how it came out, you and Jackson did an impressive piece of detective work. If it's those Hardy Boy books, maybe they should be required reading for our police force," Mr. Curcio said.

Phillip smiled weakly.

"Jackson told me everything," young Gina said. "I think you're cool, Phillip."

"And I insist that you eat. Here," Mrs. Curcio said as she placed a plate in front of Phillip.

Phillip began to eat while the Curcio family exchanged stories about embarrassing episodes in their lives. Ben told about not paying attention and walking out of the locker room naked and running into his history teacher, Mrs. Swanson. Jackson reminded Phillip about the time she made a dinner for her scout troop to earn a cooking badge, and she served cabbage instead of lettuce in the salad. Mr. Curcio told about when he was a kid giving a speech at their Thanksgiving Assembly. He had been sick the night before, but his mother had made him go to school anyway so that he could give his speech. He was feeling incredibly nervous and a little sick, and as he opened his mouth to say his first word, he threw up in front of everyone. It was pretty humiliating. Phillip did begin to feel better. The Curcio's could always cheer him up.

The whole family wanted to know every detail of Phillip's investigation. They all laughed when he told them about saying he was looking for a Dalmatian. Otherwise, they were impressed at his creative problem solving.

"Most of the good ideas were Jackson's," Phillip said. "If I had told her everything, maybe she would have figured out the real story and saved a lot of trouble."

"So, no secrets next time, promise?" Jackson said.

"I promise."

"Am I now supposed to feel safer?" Ben teased his sister.

"Absolutely," she answered confidently.

"Thanks for the meal, Mrs. Curcio," Phillip said.

"Dad cooked it," Jackson said.

"Thanks," Phillip said to Jackson's father. "I'd better get home and at least have dessert with my own family."

Phillip slowly made his way through the yard and to his back door. He just didn't want to face Mike. Mike must think that he was a bigger fool than ever. Mike hadn't really said anything yet. Phillip walked through the front doorway. Mike and Dara were on the couch watching television while Emily lay out-stretched on the living room floor, attempting to reach for a plastic rattle.

"Phillip, I saved some dinner for you," Dara said.

"I ate next door."

A hurt expression flashed on Dara's face.

"But I didn't have dessert, Mom. What do you have?"

"Root beer floats," Dara answered, smiling. "Let me make one up for you." Dara left the room.

It was now just Phillip and Mike. Emily was there, too, but she didn't count. Phillip was afraid to even glance in Mike's direction. He looked around the room awkwardly, fighting the urge to see if Mike was looking at him.

"Phillip, I'm sorry about the whole thing."

Phillip looked at Mike. Mike seemed genuinely concerned.

"I know that it's going to be tough with the other kids. You gotta expect that after what you did. I wish that you'd let me help."

"How can you help, Mike?"

"I think that the guys might have a little more respect for you if your ball playing improved."

Phillip rolled his eyes.

"I mean it!" Mike insisted. "I know what kids are like. It wasn't that long ago that I was a kid. What's wrong with my idea?"

"Mike, I'm never going to be even a decent ball player. At least most of the guys thought I was smart. They won't even think that now. I'm nothing."

"Phillip, give me a chance. What can it hurt? If you're right and you don't get any better, you're no worse off than now. Let's give it a shot. I'd kind of like to see you help put it to the Pharmacy next time you play them. That cop Cable made me sick."

"Really?"

"What a jerk. Nothing would make me happier than seeing you show up his kid on the field."

Phillip wanted that more than anything himself.

"Okay," Phillip agreed.

"You want to play some ball now?" Mike asked, surprised and pleased.

"Yeah."

"Get your glove and let's go in the yard and start with a game of catch."

Dara entered the room with a root beer float in her hand.

"Put that in the fridge for a bit," Mike said as he and Phillip headed for the back door. "We're going out for some baseball."

Dara beamed.

CHAPTER 15

Phillip decided to walk home from school instead of taking the bus. He wanted some time to think. Also, he'd taken enough guff from the other kids that he didn't want to face them on the bus. It had been a pretty bad day. Of course, everyone knew about the story. Phillip was the laughing stock of the whole school. That evening was a baseball practice. It would not be easy. He needed a little time now away from other kids.

Yesterday, in one hour with Mike, Phillip felt that his catching and throwing did improve some, especially his catching. Mike had showed him how to turn his glove when the ball came to his left. Catching it backhand, it was called. After a lot of practice, he had begun to do it automatically. Maybe the practice wouldn't be so bad, Phillip thought.

As Phillip walked home he passed Jake's Sport's Card Shop. Jake was always a good guy to talk to when a kid needed a sympathetic ear. Phillip went in the store.

"Hi, Jake."

"Hello, Phillip."

Phillip spent a few minutes poking around the shop.

"So, how's your serious situation going? The one that you wanted advice about?"

"I did what you said, Jake, and your advice was good, but it sort of backfired." Phillip ended out telling Jake the whole story.

"Phillip, you did do right. That's quite a story. You just got a bad break. It's like in baseball, you can do it all right and it just goes wrong. About the hardest hit I ever saw in a game was a rocket at the shortstop. Men were on first and second at the time. The runners were going on the pitch, a hit and run. The shortstop caught it in the air, tagged one runner coming into second and stepped on second base to double off the other runner. A triple play, unassisted! The next day, a cheap bloop single will win a game. That's just life."

"I guess it's kind of like you, Jake. You did everything right, and some bigger, fancier store knocks you clean out of business. When will you close?"

"In a couple of months, probably. They're trying to lease the place out to another business. I'm here at half rent until that happens. They figure half rent is better than nothing. I'll have a months notice, then you'll see the sale of all sales. And you'll have first shot at the stuff."

Phillip's eyes lit up. "Will your Casey Stengels be on sale?" Casey Stengel was considered the greatest manager of all time. Casey Stengel and John McGraw were Phillip's favorites.

"Everything will."

Phillip suddenly felt guilty for being excited about Jake going out of business. His smile disappeared.

"Don't feel bad," Jake said. "Nothing will make me happier than to have you get something good out of this."

"Hey Jake, how come Cards and Comics can sell All-Star signed uniforms for only fifty bucks?"

"I don't know how they can do a lot of things, Phillip. Maybe they're taking a loss until I go out of business, then they'll jack up their prices and there'll be no one to compete with them. Or maybe they're selling lots of fake stuff. Maybe you should focus some of your investigative prowess on that questionable outfit."

Maybe I should, Phillip thought.

"Wait a minute. I see that look in your eye. I was just kidding. I'm retiring and that's that. You stay out of it. I want to retire. I'm ready for a change."

He didn't look like he meant it, Phillip thought.

"I have to go now, Jake. I have a practice soon."

"Bye, Phillip."

"Bye."

Phillip was no longer worrying about facing his teammates at practice. It was much more important that he help Jake. Jake needed his help. There must be something illegal going on for Cards and Comics Superstore to make some of their deals. There was no question in Phillip's mind.

When he got home, he looked at his watch. Four o'clock. He had an hour before his practice. When practice was at five o'clock, his parents always had a later dinner. They'd let him snack well beforehand. But instead of going into his own house, he went straight to Jackson's. She was in her yard shooting baskets with Gina. They had a basket with an adjustable height. Jackson had it at its lowest setting for Gina. Phillip saw Gina pass the ball to Jackson who dribbled and stuffed it in the short basket. Gina cheered her sister. Jackson looked up, beaming, then saw Phillip.

"Phillip, how come you weren't on the bus this afternoon?"

"I needed to walk home."

Jackson didn't have to ask why. She knew. Even Jackson had taken some teasing today in school about the whole cat thing. And the kids almost never teased Jackson. It didn't seem to bother her, though. She had told Phillip that she knew they had done the right thing. Phillip knew what she said was true, but it still bothered him when the other kids laughed. He wished that he could be more like Jackson.

"Hey, Jackson, I need to talk to you," Phillip said.

"What's up?"

"It kind of has to be just you and me." Phillip shot a glance at Jackson's little sister.

"Gina, you work on your jump shot. I'll be back later," Jackson said as she threw Gina a bounce pass.

Phillip followed Jackson into her house and up to her room. He shut the door as he entered.

"Ooh, what's so top secret? Another murder to report?" Jackson asked, her eyes laughing.

"You'll never believe this, but it is sort of like that. But it's not a murder."

"What is it? Tell me. Everything this time."

"I will. I won't be alone on this one. I need your help."

"So? Are you going to keep me in suspense all day?"

"No. It's about Jake's Sport's Cards. You know how Jake is going out of business?"

"Yeah. You told me that. That's too bad. He's a nice guy."

"Well, it's all because of Cards and Comics Superstore."

"Sure, like when Arnie's Corner Drug Store went out of business when the Pharmacy came to town. Big stores always do that to little stores. Like the food chain."

"There's more to this, though. I'm almost sure that Cards and Comics has been doing something illegal to sell things for such low prices. If we find out and they get caught, then Jake can stay in business. We have to help him."

"Haven't we learned our lesson?" Jackson asked with a gleam in her eye.

"So you don't want to help?"

"Not at all. It sounds like great fun!"

"We need to work fast, Jackson. Jake could be out of his shop and closed down any day. They're trying to lease the store property to another business. When they do, he's gone."

"Then what are we waiting for? Let's get started! What do we do first?"

"We need to poke around a little at Cards and Comics. Learn as much as we can."

"Let's go!"

"I have a practice at five."

"So when do we go?"

"They close at seven. So we'll have to do it right after school tomorrow. We can walk home instead of taking the bus."

"Okay, tomorrow, after school. Cards and Comics."

CHAPTER 16

"It's him!" Phillip heard one player call out. There followed a chorus of comments from the other players.

"There he is."

"The saber man."

"The baseball detective."

"Baseball sleuth."

"I like that, the baseball sleuth. He's sure not a player." Sleuth was another name for a detective. Phillip's teammates all laughed.

"Enough!" Coach Higgins growled. Coach Higgins wasn't trying to be nice to Phillip. He hated it when anything distracted the team from its only real purpose: playing baseball.

"Crafts, out in right field," he ordered Phillip.

"Phillip, they say that you've figured out who was behind the assassination of John Kennedy. Is that true?" Harry asked, laughing at him.

"Shut up," Phillip said.

"Why? What are you going to do about it? Get me arrested?"

"Leave him alone, Harry," Maggie said. Phillip felt relieved. Not everyone was against him. "He has more important things on his mind, like the Lindberg kidnapping," she continued.

Even Maggie was ridiculing Phillip, and she usually didn't. The kidnapping of the Lindberg baby was the biggest unsolved crime of the century. All the fifth graders in Centerville had learned about Lindberg in History class. Charles Lindberg was the most famous aviator of all time. He was the first to fly across the Atlantic Ocean alone. Afterwards, someone kidnapped his baby from his house. No one ever found out who did it.

Phillip got in right field. When Coach Higgins hit one to him, he never even took the two steps in to get under the ball. It just plopped in front of his feet. After working with Mike, it was a ball that he could have caught. But not now. His mind just wasn't on baseball.

Forget about the past, Phillip told himself. Jackson wouldn't let the taunts bother her. I won't either. But it wasn't so easy when even Jamien called out, "Figure out how you missed that one, sleuth." And Jamien was as bad as he was!

After fielding practice, it was time for hitting. When it was Phillip's turn to go to the plate, Art tossed him a toy magnifying glass and said, "This should help you keep your eye on the ball. It sounds like you need one of these from what I hear."

Phillip let it fall to the ground as he stepped up to hit. He swung at and missed the first three pitches. The fourth was a dribbler to the mound. After two more misses, Coach Higgins yelled, "Next!"

All the other kids had gotten at least ten pitches! It wasn't fair, Phillip thought. But Coach Higgins wasn't a man you argued with.

Only Lars actually asked Phillip something and bothered to listen to him. Sitting together on the bench, Lars asked, "Phillip, did you really tell the police that a guy murdered an old lady, but it was really just a cat?"

"Not quite, but almost."

"That's a doozy. My parents would've wrecked me if I did that. What about yours?"

"They were all right, actually."

"Lars, pay attention!" Coach Higgins barked.

He didn't yell at me, Phillip thought. Usually, that's a good thing. But Phillip figured it meant that it didn't matter if he paid attention. He was lousy anyway. Lars mattered.

The practice seemed like an especially long one to Phillip. Finally it was over.

"Three more games this season," the coach told the team at the end of practice. "If we can win at least two, we end out with a winning record. Otherwise, it will be my first losing season as a coach. And I won't tolerate that. The final game of the season is against the Pharmacy. I do want to win that one. We're a better team. We never had a chance to prove it last time."

The kids all stared at Phillip. A few whispered 'sleuth.'

"See you on Thursday," Coach Higgins said as a way of dismissing the team.

Phillip walked home by himself.

"How was practice?" Dara asked as he walked in the door.

"Fine," he said quietly. He didn't feel like going into it with her.

Dara was holding a happy Emily. Emily was sucking on a cloth diaper which Dara used throughout the day to clean up her drool and spit-up. They called it her spit rag. Phillip realized that Emily hadn't been crying so much lately. Maybe the colic was ending. His mom had seemed in better moods as well. But too much had been going on with Phillip for him to care much.

That evening was a long one. Phillip couldn't get his mind off his assignment for the next day. After dinner, he played a little more ball with Mike. They played catch in the front yard, then went across the street to Andrews Field, where Mike gave Phillip some batting practice. Between pitches, Mike often had advice to share. He stressed keeping the back foot down and making a good, level swing. And he reminded Phillip many times to keep his eye on the ball so he could actually see the bat hit the ball. Unfortunately, Phillip usually missed the ball, so he couldn't see that contact. By the end of his hitting, he was able to connect with many of Mike's slow pitches, but when he speeded it up, like he'd see in Little League, it was hard for him to connect at all. But he did feel that he was getting better. Then Mike hit outfield fungoes to Phillip. Mike used a long, skinny bat with a very thin handle and a fat end, and hit Phillip fly balls out of his hand. Phillip missed every one of them. Even if it went right at him and he got his glove on it, it still fell out. Mike was encouraging, and said catching real batted flies took a lot of practice. Maybe when I can concentrate more I'll be better, Phillip thought. Mike said that a guy can learn a lot of baseball in two weeks, which was when the Pizza House Braves played the Pharmacy Phillies.

After baseball with Mike, Phillip returned home, did his homework, and went to bed. Maybe the night would go by faster if he went to bed early.

CHAPTER 17

"Phillip, over here!" Jackson called, waving from the sidewalk near their bus.

"Hi, Jackson. Ready?"

"You bet."

"You coming?" Al, the bus driver called to Phillip and Jackson.

"No, we're walking today," Jackson answered.

Al waved, closed the bus door and drove off.

"What are we looking for at Cards and Comics?" Jackson asked as they started off to the store.

"Anything suspicious. Also look for where they keep their records. That's what we really want, to see their records. We just need to, sort of, uh..."

"Case the joint," Jackson finished his sentence.

"That's right," Phillip said, and laughed. That's an expression that bad guys in old movies and TV shows use when they are checking out a place like a bank that they want to rob. "I'll try talking to the owner about his business, like I'm impressed. We'll be buddies after a while."

The two of them walked the rest of the way in silence with Jackson sometimes almost running to keep up with Phillip's fast stride. They turned a final corner and there it was, Cards and Comics Superstore. A huge sign hung above the front window. Phillip and Jackson crossed the street and approached the front door. It was a heavy glass door with a shiny, modern silver frame. There were no notices taped on the glass. A buzzer sounded as they entered. They were greeted inside by a sign which warned, 'Shoplifting Is a Crime and Will Be Prosecuted.' Another sign warned them that the premises were filmed by hidden cameras. There were no signs like those at Jake's.

Phillip tried to scan the entire store. It was huge, clean, well organized and brightly lit. And it was unfriendly too. It was everything Jake's store wasn't. One whole wall was filled with individual baseball cards. Phillip headed in that direction. For older cards, Phillip noticed sections for each decade. The 70's, the 60's, the 50's, etc...Those older cards were all inside a glass casing, probably so kids couldn't steal the expensive ones. Then he noticed another section behind the glass counter below, one he had never seen before in any card shop. Managers! There were Sparky Andersons, Earl Weavers, Yogi Berras, Joe Torres, Tony LaRussas, and a whole row of Casey Stengels! Underneath Stengel, there was an old Leo Durocher selling for $300! The card looked practically new, but it had to have been at least fifty years old. Someone must have kept it saved in an unopened pack with bubble gum. Phillip imagined how hard the gum must have been when it was finally opened.

"Can I see the Durocher there?" Phillip asked the man nearby. Phillip guessed that the man was the owner.

"You're seeing it now, aren't you?" the tall, balding man growled.

"Can I hold it?"

"It wouldn't be in that mint condition if I let kids like you paw it." The man used to have black hair, but now most of it was gone. There was a little around his ears, and a few long strands draped across his bald head. "Do you want to buy it?"

"Maybe," Phillip answered. "Are you the owner?"

"I work here. What does it matter to you if I'm the owner. You want a card, I'll sell it to you."

This wasn't going to be easy, Phillip thought. His friendly conversation strategy was not working. Time for fast thinking.

"Uh, I want to see the owner. It's about getting a job here."

"You? You can't be more than twelve years old!"

"No, my brother is looking for a part time job," Jackson piped in. Phillip didn't even know Jackson was standing nearby and listening.

"Well, we don't need any new workers."

"I'd like to talk to the owner and hear that," Jackson insisted.

"I am the owner."

"What's your name?" Jackson asked with authority.

"Schmidt. Ray Schmidt. Mr. Schmidt to you."

"Mr. Schmidt," Phillip said, "some kids on my team said that you have signed uniforms from last year's all-star teams."

"Yeah. Over there." Mr. Schmidt pointed to another glass case near the front of the store.

"Do you have a Nomar Garciaparra?"

"I'm out. I sold three of them this week."

"Ken Griffey Jr?"

"I'm out of him, too. I sold the two I had of him. Anyone else you want?"

"Naw, just those guys."

"I might have some coming in later this week. Try then, or leave me your name and number, and I'll call you if I get something."

"I'll come back," Phillip said. "Do you buy cards?"

"No, we just sell them."

"Can I see a signed uniform?"

"Sure. Over here, kid."

Schmidt led Phillip to a glass cabinet. He unlocked it and pulled out a baseball shirt signed by someone.

"Who's that? I can't read the writing."

"Wade Boggs."

"How much?"

"Seventy-five."

"I heard they were fifty!"

"Future hall-of-famers are seventy five."

Phillip examined the shirt carefully. "How do I know that Boggs really signed it?"

"You get a certificate of authentication with it."

Phillip nodded. "I think I'll just look around a little more."

"Just don't mess with the expensive stuff, kid."

Phillip looked around for another half hour. He occasionally crossed paths with Jackson. At one point, after he had spent five minutes looking at manager cards, Jackson approached from behind and elbowed him.

"Sorry," he whispered, realizing that he was supposed to be working, not playing. He got busy again 'casing the joint.'

Phillip and Jackson finally nodded to each other and left.

"Anything interesting?" Phillip asked Jackson as soon as they got out the door.

"Yeah. I saw four sales made. On two of them, the woman at the cash register didn't ring up the sale. She just hit $0.00 and figured out the change in her head."

"That means that they're probably cheating on their taxes. My father told me about that trick."

"And that woman," Jackson said, "she's married to the guy you were talking to, Schmidt, the owner. He looks older, though. And they have a little boy, about two years old."

"How'd you know that? Did she tell you?"

"No. She had a picture cube at the front counter. Ray Schmidt, the woman and the kid were all together, like they were a family. The other pictures were of the kid. And they probably live above the store."

"How'd you know that?"

"As we walked in, I noticed there was an apartment above the store. Usually an owner of a new business would want to live there. And there's a child's room sticker on a window. That's in case there's a fire, the firemen check that room first. What about you, what did you notice?"

"I'm suspicious. For one thing, they don't buy cards. That's unusual for a baseball card shop. And these signed baseball shirts are too good a deal to be true. My dad used to say, if it sounds too good to be true, it usually is. The other thing that makes me suspicious is that the guy said he could get a Nomar or a Junior signed shirt in a few days if I wanted one. That doesn't sound right. You don't just order those like new baseballs. I'd like to see those certificates of authentication."

"What are those, Phillip?"

"It's something that guarantees the signatures are real."

"What guarantees the certificate is true?" Jackson asked.

"I don't know. Probably nothing. But I'd like to see one anyway. A bunch of the guys on my team bought shirts from there. I can borrow a certificate from one of them."

"You think anyone on the team will lend you anything these days?"

"Lars will. He bought one."

"And I have an idea, too. I think that I can get into their house when they're not around. That way, I can really explore."

"Jackson, you're not going to break in there! That's too dangerous!"

"No, I'm not going to break in."

"Then how're you going to do it?" Phillip asked.

"Watch." Jackson turned around and headed back to Cards and Comics. Phillip followed. She marched right back into the store with Phillip just behind. She walked straight up to Ray Schmidt.

"Mr. Schmidt?"

"Back so soon?" he asked.

"Mr. Schmidt, I have a business proposal."

"Yes?"

"I'm eleven years old. I turn twelve next month. I have one lit-tle sister that I watch a lot, and my parents just gave me per-mission to baby-sit for other kids. You have a little kid, right?"

"Yeah?" he asked suspiciously.

"The kid probably drives you crazy at times, like all little kids do, and it's good to get away for a while, just you and Mrs. Schmidt. I want to start a sitting business. I'm good. How would you like to hire me?"

"We already have a sitter we use. And we don't get out too often anyway. It gets too expensive with what you guys charge these days."

"I'm better than your other sitter. I'm so sure, Mr. Schmidt, that if I sit and you don't ever want me to sit again, I'm free. You don't pay! How can you resist that deal? Besides, I only charge $3.00 an hour. That's cheap around here."

"It is. And your deal is tempting. Let me talk for a minute with the missus."

Ray Schmidt walked over to his wife and spoke quietly with her for a minute. They came back together.

"What's your name?" Mrs. Schmidt asked.

"Jackson. Jackson Curcio. My real name is Jacqueline Sonya but everyone calls me Jackson."

"Ray said you have a younger brother?"

"Sister. She's seven."

"My Luke is four years old. You seem like a pretty on-the-ball kid. Can you sit on Friday night?"

"Sure," Jackson said, trying to hide her joy.

"Seven o'clock?"

"I'll be here."

"I can get you. Where do you live?"

"Next to Andrews Field. But I can get here myself. You can drive me home later. What time will you need me till?"

"About eleven," Mrs. Schmidt said.

"Great."

"Just write down your phone number here in case something comes up. If you need to call me, just call the store. We live right upstairs. The number is the same."

Jackson wrote down her number and handed it to Mrs. Schmidt.

"Friday, then," Mrs. Schmidt said and smiled.

"Friday."

Jackson left the store, followed by Phillip.

"That was awesome," Phillip said.

Jackson beamed.

CHAPTER 18

"How's it going?" Phillip asked over the phone.

"Not so great. I haven't gotten too much of a chance to look around. This kid is kind of a brat."

"I'm not surprised."

"First, they didn't leave until a half hour ago, about seven-thirty," Jackson said. "I had to just hang out and wait for them to get ready. It was pretty awkward because when Luke would squawk, I didn't know if I was supposed to deal with him or if his parents should. I was glad when they left."

"So, what about then? Didn't you get a chance to check things out?" Phillip asked. Phillip was using his parents' phone, where he was less likely to be overheard.

"I tried popping a movie into the VCR. That usually works, but every five minutes he changed his mind about what he wanted to see. There's a whole bookcase full of videos. Every one ever created for kids."

"Where are you calling from?"

"I'm in the kitchen. Luke is in the living room. There's lots of fighting in the movie he's watching now. Karate and stuff."

"What one is it?" Phillip asked over the phone.

"How should I know? All those stupid things are the same."

"No they're not."

"Phillip, let's not argue about that now. Hey, how'd your game turn out?"

"We lost, 6-2."

"Was Higgins bummed?"

"A little, but we were playing the Petro Plus Dodgers."

"So?"

"There're in first place. Even Coach Higgins didn't expect we'd beat them. But if we win the last two, we end up over five hundred."

"Five hundred wins? You haven't played that many games!"

"No, Jackson. A five-hundred winning percentage. Point five-oh-oh. That means we win more than we lose."

"How did *you* do?"

"I got my first hit of the season! Actually it was kind of an error, but I got on first, and it was against Billy McGrath. I bunted, and the catcher had a hard time picking it up. They said he looked like a juggler bobbling the ball. I wish I had seen it."

"You didn't see it?"

"No, I was too busy running hard to first base. You're not supposed to look at the ball. Just run hard and watch the first base coach."

"That's great, Phillip. Mike must have been proud of you."

"He wasn't there," Phillip said sadly into the phone. "He had his own softball game again. He's working during our game against the Giants on Wednesday, too. But he'll be able to come next weekend for our last game, against the Pharmacy. I think that he wants us to win that one even more than I do. He can't stand that policeman Cable."

"Maybe there's hope for him after all. Anyone who hates Cable can't be all bad."

"Mike's been okay recently. And he has helped me a lot with my game. I'm still pretty bad, but a higher level of bad than before. And I've had fun with him," Phillip said, and paused.

"So, when does the kid go to bed? You still want me to come over when he's asleep?"

"Definitely. I need help, particularly with the baseball stuff. You know all about that."

"What time?" Phillip asked.

"Mrs. Schmidt said about eight-fifteen. But Mr. Schmidt laughed and said 'That'll be a first.' So I don't know. He definitely won't be in bed in fifteen minutes. We have until eleven o'clock, so we should be okay."

"Yeah, but I want to be out of there by ten-thirty. I wish that you'd asked if I could come too."

"No way. I probably never would have gotten in at all. Parents don't trust two kids together, especially if one is a boy and one is a girl, and certainly not on the first time you sit. It had to be this way."

Phillip knew Jackson was right.

"Jackson!" Phillip heard a little kid scream from the distance. It must be Luke. He was probably bored with the karate movie.

"Phillip, I gotta go. Call me about eight-thirty. Hopefully, he'll be in bed then and you can come over. Meanwhile, I'll see what I can find out."

"Okay, good luck."

"Thanks. Bye, Phillip."

"Bye."

Phillip hung up, then picked up his latest mystery, *The Missing School.* It was about a school which had just disappeared. Most of the kids were thrilled that there was no more school, but the smart kid in the class knew how important school was and tried to find the school. The kid suspected that aliens were trying to take over the earth by getting rid of all schools and making the humans stupid. It was a pretty dumb story, but Phillip could identify with the kid detective, and so he liked it anyway. But it was tough concentrating on his reading with his real life mystery happening at the same time.

After a while, Phillip put his book down and picked up Lars's certificate of authentication for his Juan Gonzales shirt. It was from a company called Sports Collectibles. There was a post office address from San Antonio, Texas. Phillip had already written, asking for more information about the company. His letter had said that he was visiting San Antonio this summer, and wanted to visit the store.

Finally, eight-thirty arrived. Phillip ran into his parents' bedroom and dialed the Schmidt's number.

"Hello?" a little kid's voice answered.

"Hello?" Jackson's voice came over the phone, at almost the same time.

"Not good, huh?" Phillip asked.

"Oh God, no."

"What about reading a bedtime story, like you do with Gina?"

"They don't have any books here, Phillip! And these movies are all full of action and get the brat wired. All he wants is junk food. If I give it to him, he gets a sugar high. If I don't, he screams. I'm surprised you haven't heard him from your house. I'm even more surprised that the police haven't showed up," Jackson said, sounding exasperated.

"Is it possible I can get in without him seeing me? Then I could try to get into the store and look around."

"That's kind of dangerous, Phillip. If he sees you and tells his parents, that'll be it. Besides, I don't even think there's a way to go straight to the store from here."

"But if I don't try to get in soon, it sounds like we're not going to get anywhere anyway."

Jackson was quiet for a moment. "I suppose you're right. Just don't ring the door bell or knock. The door to their house is on the left side of the store. You walk in the door and go up a flight of stairs. When can you get here?"

"Fifteen minutes."

"I'll check the door at ten of nine. Just wait there. If you're not here by then, I'll just check every ten minutes after that," Jackson said.

"Let's synchronize our watches." In mysteries, police always made sure their watches were set to the exact same time. "What time do you have?" Phillip asked.

"Eight thirty-four."

"Got ya. See you soon."

"Mom, I'm going next door to Jackson's," Phillip called as he went out the door.

"What time will you be back?" Dara called back to him from the front window.

"Around ten?"

"It's a weekend, I guess so. Just not much later, though."

It was too dark to bike. Phillip ran instead. The Schmidt's house was above Cards and Comics and was about a mile away. It took Phillip a little more than fifteen minutes to get there. It was too far to run all the way, and so he mixed walking with running. The door to the house was exactly where Jackson had said. Phillip entered. He was in a dark hallway and felt a little scared as the outside door closed. Phillip felt along the wall for a light switch, but couldn't find one. He reached back to find the door again, but he couldn't find that! Oh, no!

After another step, Phillip at last did put his hand on the door and he turned the knob and opened it. Enough light came in from the streetlights outside that Phillip finally did spot the light switch. It was on the left side of the door. Funny place to put it. Phillip switched on the light and walked up the stairs. There was one door at the top. He checked his watch. Eight fifty-three. He sat down and watched each minute change on his digital watch. When the number read eight fifty-nine, the door opened. It was Jackson.

Jackson put her right index finger to her lips, quietly whis-pering, "Shh."

Shooting and screaming sounded from the TV in the other room. Jackson directed Phillip to follow. He walked behind her, into an adult bedroom. When they were both inside, Jackson closed the door.

"What's he watching now?" Phillip asked.

"Cowboys and Indians. An oldie. Why don't you go get your pajamas and join him? He'd love your PJs."

Phillip felt his face turn red with embarrassment.

"I just gave him a bowl full of gummy bears," Jackson said. "Those things take forever to chew. He should be quiet and happy for quite a while."

"Then let's start here," Phillip said. "I'll look in the bureaus and you can look in the closets. Leave everything exactly as you find it!"

"Of course!" Jackson said and made a smirking face at Phillip.

Phillip opened the top drawer of the bigger bureau. A lady's underwear and bras. It must be Mrs. Schmidt's dresser. Suddenly, Phillip felt funny about looking through someone else's things. What if these people are innocent, too? They'd be really angry to have some kid searching their stuff. Phillip remembered how he felt when Mike had searched his room for the saber saw.

"Is what we're doing all right?" Phillip asked Jackson.

Jackson stopped looking through the closet. "I was thinking the same thing myself. It doesn't feel right. I don't know. Police look through people's houses, don't they?"

"That's true," Phillip said, "but they usually have a search warrant."

"We can't exactly do that, now, can we? We're just kids."

"Right. But if the police suspect someone committed a crime, then they can get a warrant to let them search. We have good reason to suspect the Schmidts, don't we?"

"I don't know, Phillip. You're the one who said that there's no way they could do those baseball deals. I don't know about any of that."

"Something's fishy, I'm sure of it."

"You were sure of the murder, too."

True. It wasn't easy. What was the right thing to do? He felt truly bad about all the heartache he had caused Robert Hallman and his family. He had written a letter of apology this week, and no one had even asked him to. His mom always said the best apologies are ones nobody forces you to make. This was a tough decision, though. Jackson looked at him, waiting for him to decide. Phillip was the police and a judge, combined, deciding if a search was warranted. And just as he was ready to chicken out and stop the whole thing, he thought of Jake. He saw Jake's kind eyes, and remembered the sadness in them when he had told Phillip the store was closing. And Jake suspected something, too. He wouldn't have said anything if he hadn't. Jake needed Phillip's help.

"Let's do it."

Phillip searched Mrs. Schmidt's bureau completely. Nothing. Just clothes. He went to the other side of the bed and began to look through the other bureau. He checked the top drawer–jockey underwear and socks. Next, he opened the second drawer.

Just then, the bedroom door opened. Phillip dove to the floor behind the bed.

"Gummy bears stuck!" a child's voice cried.

"Gummy bears are stuck in your teeth?"

"Yes."

Phillip lay flat on the floor, not moving a muscle. He saw two bare feet standing on the other side of the bed. And he noticed a box under the bed, up against the wall to his right. While he prayed that the little boy wouldn't come around the bed, he also wondered what was in that box. Maybe documents. Evidence of forgeries or other crimes. Things you might want to hide under your bed.

"Come on, I'll help," Jackson said.

She walked out of the bedroom with little Luke and closed the door behind her. Phillip breathed a deep sigh of relief. His heart was still pounding. He reached under the bed, and pulled out the flat, cardboard box. Every nerve in his body tingled with excitement as he prepared to open it. This might contain the evidence he needed to save Jake's store! Slowly, Phillip removed the cover and peeked inside. Toy rattles. Baby clothes. Other baby toys. Just old baby stuff, Phillip thought, almost wanting to cry from disappointment. He reached in and picked up some of the clothes. More baby stuff: bottles, tiny stuffed animals, a Snuggly pouch for carrying babies, a set of baby monitors...monitors! Baby monitors!

Phillip knew just what to do. It was too good to be true!

A minute later, Jackson opened the door and walked in.

"Look!" Phillip shouted.

"Old baby stuff, so what?"

"Look here, a baby monitor!"

"So?"

"Don't you see, Jackson? We can hide one half in the house, and take the other half with us. If they're doing something illegal, we're sure to hear them talk about it. This is it! We can load in batteries and this will definitely lead us to the evidence we need."

One look at Jackson and it was clear that she agreed.

CHAPTER 19

Bob Hennessy of the Concrete Giants took off his cap and wiped the sweat from his forehead. Phillip stepped out of the batters box. The count was two balls and one strike. Phillip looked to third for the signal. Coach Higgins adjusted his cap, then nodded. Phillip nodded back. They were using new signals. It was the green light! Coach Higgins, who had given him the red light on a 3 and 2 count just two games ago, was letting him swing! Phillip had been connecting better in batting practice. The extra work with Mike must be the difference, Phillip thought. Bob Hennessy had good control but couldn't throw very hard. That was Phillip's favorite kind of pitcher. That was most hitters' favorite kind of pitcher. That's why the Braves were on top 7-1 in the fourth. Phillip stepped into the batters box and gripped the bat tightly. Please throw it over the plate. I don't want a walk. I want a hit. I can hit this guy. Hennessy looked at the runner on third, then back at Phillip. He wound up and pitched. Smash! Phillip dropped the bat and ran as hard as he could to first base. He crossed the bag but there was no signal from the first base coach. Should he stay or make the turn to second? Phillip turned around to see what had happened. The Concrete Giants were jogging towards their dugout. Phillip looked again at Mr. Clark who was coaching first base.

"What happened?"

"Nice hit, Phillip. Line drive to short. Art was picked off at third for a double play."

He had hit into a double play! How could he do that? This was his chance to really prove something. Phillip walked back to the dugout with his head low. His two innings were up and his coach would surely pull him out now. Especially after a double play.

"Great hit, Crafts. Tough luck. Get out in the field, on the double!" Coach Higgins barked.

Phillip grabbed his glove and sprinted to his position. On his way out, he passed Art, who was brushing the dirt from his uniform.

"Nice hit," Art said as Phillip went by.

Phillip stood out in right field, and it didn't matter that he didn't get a single ball that inning. He had cracked the ball, and the kids were impressed, even if it was a double play. Even Art had said 'Good hit.' Jake was right. Sometimes you crack it and do it all right and you're out. I guess that's fair, Phillip thought. Last time I hit a bad bunt and got on when the catcher couldn't pick it up.

Phillip got up one more time, this time against Harvey Prescott. Harvey was the opposite of Billy. Harvey threw hard but had poor control, but Phillip didn't care. He walked up to the plate, sure that he could hit anyone, even Harvey. Coach Higgins gave Phillip the green light on the first two pitches. Both were in the dirt for balls. Coach Higgins flashed the red light, and Phillip nodded, agreeing with the call. The pitch came in: high and outside, ball three. Phillip stepped out of the box. He looked for the red light again. The coach flashed the sign. Red light. Good call, Phillip thought. I wouldn't have swung anyway. Harvey wound up and pitched. Fastball, strike one. Phillip turned towards third base and looked at his coach. Coach Higgins adjusted his cap. Red light. Harvey Prescott wound up. Outside corner. "Strike!" the ump called. Full count. Phillip looked once more for the signal. Green light, please. Let me hit this guy. I'm not afraid, Phillip thought. I can hit him! From the coaching box at third, Higgins adjusted his cap. Yes! The green light! Phillip would get to swing! Harvey glared at Phillip. Phillip smiled coolly in return. Harvey wound up and fired. Phillip swung as hard as he could. He missed. Strike three.

He walked back to the dugout, threw down his batting helmet and sat down on the hard wooden bench. Coach Higgins came over to him and squatted in front of him. He put his hand on Phillip's shoulder.

"That was a nice cut, Phillip. That guy's fast. Next time, with two strikes against a fastballer like that, try choking up and just meeting the ball."

Phillip nodded. Coach Higgins is treating me like one of the real players, Phillip thought. Even though he had just struck out, his heart was exploding with happiness. Maybe there was hope for him after all.

Phillip played four innings in all, the most Coach Higgins had ever played him. His Pizza House Braves beat the Giants easily, 10-3. They were 8-8 on the season. If they could beat the Pharmacy on Sunday, they'd be above .500 for the year. And they'd finish by beating Cable's team. That's all Phillip could think of during the handshake. Then he looked up at his opponents as they each touched his hand, saying 'Good game' as they always did. But they seemed to be really mean it today when they said it to Phillip. He felt good.

"Great game, Phillip," Dara said when she met him after the handshake. Emily was in Dara's arms and was beaming at her brother.

"Thanks, Mom."

"Do you have homework, Phillip? I thought we could read or something tonight. Emily's been better in the evenings lately."

"Thanks, but I'm working on a project with Jackson." He had been ready for this.

"What's it on?"

"Search and seizure. It's about search warrants and privacy."

"Sounds interesting. I can't wait to read it."

"It's an oral report, Mom. You'll hear it all, I promise."

"Good," Dara said and smiled. "No more secrets."

Phillip said nothing. He did feel a little guilty, though, but what choice did he have?

"I'm going straight to Jackson's. Take my glove?"

"Sure, hon. Don't be late."

Phillip ran to Jackson's house.

"Hi, Gina. Hi, Ben," he said as he barged through their back door. He ran right up to Jackson's room.

"Hi, Jackson," Phillip said. "Did you listen at all tonight?"

"For an hour. Nothing. It sounded like Ray was out. Anne was home alone with Luke, and so mostly I listened to Luke's videos."

"Where'd you listen from?"

"I sat on the sidewalk in front of Fast Mart, pretending I was listening to a walkman or something. I held it to my ear, and moved to the beat, just as if I were listening to music."

"Should we both go and listen together for a while?"

"Yes!"

"Dad, we're going over to Phillip's. Be back soon," Jackson called out.

"Have fun," Mr. Curcio called back.

CHAPTER 20

"Sounds like it was a great game," Jackson said as she trotted to keep up with Phillip.

"It was," Phillip said absent-mindedly as he spotted cards and Comics in the distance.

Their attention turned to their work ahead. Yesterday Phillip had listened to the monitor for an hour. Nothing important had been said. Ray Schmidt was usually out, and when he was in, they just watched TV. Jackson had hidden the monitor in the kitchen, under the sink. Phillip had thought that the living room would be best, but Jackson convinced him that they'd be less likely to have a serious conversation with the TV on. And the TV was always on. During a meal, they might talk. Phillip had agreed. Maybe the Ray Schmidt and his wife talked in their bedroom at night. Phillip and Jackson had considered putting the monitor in the bedroom, but they both felt uncomfortable about invading the Schmidts' privacy there. The kitchen would have to do.

"Where should we go to listen?" Phillip asked as they approached the Schmidt's store. "You can't go much further than across the street with this monitor."

"We'll look pretty suspicious anywhere on the street now, especially after these past two days. I say we go in their garage and listen from there. They don't lock it."

"I don't know, Jackson. That's pretty dangerous."

"So is the street. Everyone's seen us hanging out here for two days. Someone's liable to call the cops. Do you want to run into Cable again? *That's* dangerous."

"Okay."

The garage was behind the store. It was getting fairly dark, and the two kids scurried around the shop and into the Schmidt's small back yard. The garage door was closed, and so Jackson led Phillip through the small walk-in door on the side. It was a single car garage, and nearly empty. There were just a few small tools hanging from the walls and a wheel barrow, lawn mower and old plastic tarp on the floor at the far end of the garage.

"Shoot!" Phillip said. "One of them must not be home."

"Why?" Jackson asked.

"No car."

"Do you know they have a car? Not everyone with a garage has a car," Jackson said.

"If they didn't keep a car here, this garage would be filled with junk. I guarantee it. Like our garage. Nobody keeps their garage this empty unless they keep their car in it."

"I guess you're right. Let's listen anyway."

Jackson turned on the monitor.

"I want more cookies!" Luke wailed.

"Last one," Mrs. Schmidt said.

"Want to bet?" Jackson whispered to Phillip.

Silence.

"More cookies!"

"No!"

Louder. *"More cookies! More cookies!"*

"This really is the last cookie, Luke, and I mean it!"

Phillip and Jackson laughed.

Clunk-drum-errrrr. It sounded like an engine went on in the garage. Suddenly the garage door began to open and bright light shone in from below the door. Car lights! They had an automatic garage door opener, and a car was outside, coming in! Instinctively, Jackson and Phillip flew out the side door and raced into the back yard, diving into the heavy bushes next to the rear of the building. Please, I hope he didn't see us, Phillip prayed. What if he did, and what if he looks in his yard? Oh no! Suddenly he had to go to the bathroom. Bad. It was worse than when he used to play hide-and-seek. Or flash-light tag. When he was very little, those games always made him pee in his pants. As a bigger kid, he still felt like it, but he could control the urge. He wasn't so sure now. Phillip had never been so scared in his life.

Jackson had turned the monitor off, and they sat motionless in the dirt against the cement foundation.

"Get outta here! Get outta here," Ray Schmidt yelled, as he slammed the small door to the garage shut.

Phillip heard Mr. Schmidt walk to the side of the shop and enter the door there.

"Phew, that was close," Jackson said.

Phillip was still so scared he couldn't say a word. Jackson turned the monitor back on. This close, the reception was loud and clear.

"Turn it down!" Phillip whispered.

Jackson did so, then said, "They wouldn't hear anyway. They're on the second floor, and it only makes noise when they talk anyway. Let's listen."

"Have you been keeping garbage in the garage?" Ray Schmidt asked.

"No, why?"

"Some huge dog or raccoon was in there. Looked as big as a wolf. I just saw a big black shape shoot out the side door when I drove in."

Thank goodness we have black shirts on the Braves, Phillip thought, as he was still in his uniform.

"I'm worried, Ray."

"About the animal?"

"No. About those uniforms. Some guy today called and said he wanted ten of those signed shirts if we could get them all with Ken Griffey's Jr.'s autograph on them. I said I wasn't sure if we could get that many or how long it would take."

"Does he know that those ones are seventy five each?"

"Yes. He said he'd pay one hundred each if we could get them in a week."

"What are we waiting for then? Did you call Ken and order them?"

"We were never going to do this many, Ray. Two or three a month. Maybe one high priced card. It was only going to be an extra two or three hundred a month for the fake stuff."

"Ten uniforms is one thousand bucks, Anne. For one phone call. Two-hundred for Ken. Eight hundred is pure profit. Just like that!"

"Ray, it was your idea to keep it small. Under 5% you said. 'As long as 95% of business is legit, we're okay.' That's what you said. It's getting too big. Let's just say we can't get them."

"You want to send Luke to that fancy pre-school Anne? This will pay for it."

"We can afford that without this, Ray!"

"We can't afford that, and the red Mustang convertible. You wanted that car as much as I did," Ray said.

"I can live without it."

"How about this. We sell those ten shirts, but take the last Mickey Mantle rookie card off the shelf. The fake cards are more dangerous than the shirts and our profit margin is less with the cards. We'll just keep that card up here until you feel more comfortable."

"You don't care what I feel. I just said that I didn't want any more shirts sold. You always do whatever you want. So just do it. I don't care."

One of them left the room. The television was turned up in the other room. The canned laughter of sitcoms sounded in the distance over the steady hush of the monitor.

"I think we've heard enough. Let's get out of here," Phillip whispered. He was so excited he couldn't believe it. He'd even forgotten about having to pee.

"Okay," Jackson said, getting up and peeking into the yard. No one there. In a minute, Phillip and Jackson were on the sidewalk, heading home. Neither could say a word for a minute.

"Wow," Jackson finally uttered.

"Yeah, wow," echoed Phillip.

"So, do we call the police now?" Jackson asked.

"Sure, let's call Detective Cable right now. He's ready to believe anything we say. The whole department would want to bust in there this second based on our word."

"Phillip, don't be so negative! You could call Officer Hardwick or Detective Stokes."

"Jackson, they like us, but they're in so much trouble over the last one, they wouldn't be able to help. And they probably wouldn't believe us either. What we have to do is get evidence. Hard evidence."

"How?" Jackson asked.

"We need to get back in there."

CHAPTER 21

"How about a game of Clue, Phillip?" Dara asked across the dining room table.

"I can't. Sorry, Mom."

"You *can't* play Clue, your favorite game?"

"It's that project I'm working on. The one with Jackson. I need to go over there again."

"Have you considered applying for a permanent change of address?" Dara asked.

"Oh, Mom," Phillip said as he twirled another forkful of spaghetti. Phillip brought it to his mouth, slurping up the pasta that didn't stay there the first time.

"That's rude, Phillip."

"Sorry," Phillip said automatically.

"Well, I can't wait to hear this report, Phillip. You've never worked so hard on a school project in your life, and you've always done a lot. This must be an important part of your grade, huh?"

Phillip hesitated. He hated lying to his mother.

"It is important, Mom. And I didn't get to do anything this afternoon."

"Yeah, we were playing ball, Dara," Mike added, with his mouth full of spaghetti.

"Can't you empty your mouth first, Mike? I have two pigs in this house."

Mike swallowed and said, "It's a male thing, dear. Anyway, Phillip is doing a great job with his baseball." Phillip beamed. "We did more hitting and outfield fungoes. He caught three fly balls. And one of them was a shot!"

"I did really well bunting, too, Mom."

"I'm happy that you guys have been able to play. I told you that Mike could help you with baseball, Phillip."

Phillip didn't answer. She was right, though.

"He's going to be all ready for the big game on Sunday, aren't you Phillip?"

"We're going to kill the Pharmacy," Phillip declared.

"Atta boy," Mike said. "And I can't wait to see the look of that jerk Cable's face when it happens."

"Boys, maybe you shouldn't take this so seriously. It's just a game."

Emily banged the tray of her baby swing.

"It is important, Dara," Mike said.

"Yeah, even Emily thinks it is. Look," Phillip added.

Emily banged harder.

They all laughed.

"I gotta go now," Phillip said as he finished his last bite of spaghetti. "I don't need dessert."

"That's okay. And I suspect that Jean Curcio makes better desserts than I do."

"Mom," Phillip whined.

"I'm only kidding. Oh, wait. There was something in the mail for you today. It was a letter that you sent which was returned. Here."

Dara handed Phillip the letter he had written to the "certificate of authentication" place, Sports Collectibles in Texas. The letter was stamped 'RETURN. Addressee unknown.'

"What's that about?" Dara asked.

"It's nothing, Mom. I just wrote to a baseball place trying to get free stuff."

"It looks like they're out of business," Dara said as Phillip was leaving the table. "Have fun."

Phillip took off. He held on to his first piece of evidence. He couldn't wait to show it to Jackson. This almost proved those certificates were fakes. He would talk to Jackson now about how to get into the house and get more evidence. The returned letter itself would not do it, but it would help. Right after school, Jackson and Phillip had gone to the store to see if they wanted Jackson to baby-sit again. That would have been easy. But Ray Schmidt had said that they would stick with their regular sitter! Jackson was sure that it was because he was so cheap and this way he wouldn't have to pay Jackson for that first time. That had been the deal. Or maybe that brat Luke had complained because Jackson didn't feed him *every* bit of junk food in the house. It was going to be tough trying to get in there some other way.

"Hi, Mrs. Curcio. Hi, Ben," Phillip greeted them.

"Phillip, where's Jackson? I thought she was with you?"

"She was earlier, but not now. I've been playing ball with Mike, and eating."

"Where could she be? She's always good about telling me where she goes, unless she's at your house. That's strange."

Phillip swallowed hard. A pit of fear formed in his stomach.

"I think I know where she is, Mrs. Curcio. Can I check her room?"

"Go ahead."

Phillip ran upstairs. There was no monitor on her desk. That was where she usually left it. He went back downstairs.

"She must be working on our project, Mrs. Curcio. I think I know where she is. Probably at the library. She can get so engrossed, it's easy to lose track of time. I'll go get her."

"Thanks, Phillip. Don't be long."

Phillip felt nervous. "If we're just about done the library part, is it all right if we stay there and finish it?"

"She hasn't eaten yet."

"You know Jackson. She'd rather finish a job first."

"That's true. Okay, just don't be too long."

"Bye," Phillip said, and left.

Phillip ran to the Schmidt's Cards and Comics Superstore and arrived there covered with sweat from both the running and the worrying. He searched the surrounding sidewalks, hoping to see Jackson listening to the monitor. No sign of her. Where could she be?

It wasn't dark enough yet, but he had to try the garage. Phillip made his way along the side of the shop, past the door leading up to their apartment, and around the building into the small yard. He glanced up at the back windows of the Schmidt second floor apartment. He prayed that no one would be looking out. It was hard to see with the glare of the late evening sun, but he didn't think he saw anyone. Here goes, he said to himself.

Phillip walked up to the side door of the garage, stepped in and closed the door behind him. Their red convertible took up nearly the whole garage. With just one window, it was a lot darker inside the garage than outside. Phillip let his eyes adjust to the darkness, then began to look around. The tarp was on top of the wheelbarrow. He picked up the piece of plastic cloth, looked in the wheelbarrow, and saw it. The monitor! Next to the monitor was Jackson's portable cassette player. She wasn't going to listen to music, was she? He picked it up and ejected the tape. It was a blank tape. He looked at the cassette player setting. The 'record' button was pushed, but nothing was happening. The tape was not at the beginning. It looked to Phillip like it was about fifteen minutes into it, about four songs worth. She must have been recording the Schmidts, hoping to get evidence, when the batteries ran out. The monitor was turned off. Phillip turned it on.

He heard Jackson whispering, *"Please Phillip. Please be listening. I'm trapped in their bedroom. They're home now, and I can't leave. I'm under their bed. I'll explain later, but I need to get out. You need to somehow get them out of the house so that I can escape. I have evidence. Just get them out."*

Pause.

She repeated, *"Phillip, if you're listening, I'm trapped in their bedroom. They're home now, and I can't leave. I'm under the bed and I need to get out. You need to get them out of the house so that I can escape. I have evidence. Just get them out."*

Pause.

"I'm here, Jackson. I hear you. I'm coming!" Phillip said to the monitor, wishing Jackson could hear him.

"Phillip, I hope you're listening..."

CHAPTER 22

How many times had she spoken that message? What's the monitor doing in the bedroom? Why did she go in? Why couldn't she have waited? We were in this together, Phillip thought.

"Think Phillip, think!" he said to himself out loud. How can he get the Schmidts out? Should he call the police now? After all that had happened, the police might not believe him. If they didn't, they would insist he keep away from the Schmidt's house. Then she'd really be in trouble. Once Jackson had disappeared for a while, then the police might listen. But he didn't have time for that. The Schmidts could discover her at any moment. If they did, who knows what they might do?

The recorder. If Phillip could get a tape of Jackson's cry for help, then he could bring that to the police, and they'd have to believe him! All he had to do was get out of the garage unseen, go to a drug store, buy new batteries for the recorder, and come back and make a tape. He would then bring that to the police. There were a lot of steps, and if one of them went wrong, like someone looking out the window when he was going in or coming out of the garage, well, that could be a disaster. It seemed the best strategy, though.

Where could he buy a battery? The Pharmacy was just two blocks away. That would be funny if the Pharmacy saved the day. But wait. He didn't have any money! It would take at least a half hour to run home and get money, then come back. And what if his parents got suspicious?

"Phillip. Please be listening. I'm trapped in their bedroom. They're home now, and I can't leave. I'm under their bed. I need to get out. You have to somehow get them out of the house so that I can escape. I have the evidence we need. Just get them out."

She kept on repeating the message.

Phillip had to try the recording. Doing anything himself was too dangerous. He opened the battery compartment of the cassette player. It took four AA batteries. He had no idea what they cost. Phillip then peeked out the door and looked at the Schmidt's back windows. No one there. He walked out of the garage and around the shop, and then out to the street. So far so good.

How else could he get money for the batteries? He looked up and down the street, searching for an idea. Art Norton lived two blocks away. Art was the last guy on the team who would lend Phillip money, but he had to try.

Phillip had been to Art's house once, about three years ago. That was when you didn't pick your friends but parents arranged play dates. Art had tried to play ball with him in the yard. Phillip had just wanted to play on their new computer. Their parents never arranged another play date for Phillip and Art.

Phillip ran to the house and rang the front door bell. Mr. Norton answered.

"Phillip!" He knew Phillip because he sometimes helped out at practices.

"Hi, Mr. Norton. Is Art there?"

"Sure, just a minute. Come on in. Hey, nice playing the other day. Your game's improved."

"Thanks. My stepfather's been working with me."

"Just a minute," Mr. Norton said, disappearing into the other room.

"Hi, Phillip," Art said, trying not to look surprised. Phillip knew Art had to be wondering why he was there.

"Art, I need a huge favor. It's *really* important. I need you to lend me some money."

"How much?"

Phillip thought for a moment. "I'm not sure, but I need to buy four AA batteries right now. I don't have time to go home and get money first. I'll do anything for them. I'll even give you my signed Tony LaRussa baseball card for this!"

Art winced. "Just a second," he said, and left the room. He returned about two minutes later.

"Here, Phillip." He handed Phillip four AA batteries. "I took them from my radio."

"Thanks! I'll give you the card tomorrow. I promise."

"You don't have to. That signed card is worth ten times what those batteries are worth. And I know it's your favorite card."

"What do you want, then?" Phillip asked.

"Just return my batteries tomorrow."

"You don't want anything else?"

"No, Phillip. We're teammates. This must be pretty important or you wouldn't offer me your LaRussa card."

Phillip wanted to cry. He felt bad about all the nasty things he had thought about Art Norton.

"Thanks, Art."

"Sure."

Phillip ran back to Cards and Comics. It was darker now, and he safely slipped back into the garage and loaded the batteries into the cassette player. Jackson was still calmly repeating the same message. It must be so hard for her, he thought, not knowing if I'm even listening. He prayed as he pressed the power button. Please work. Oh, please work. The red light went on! It worked!

Phillip rewound the tape and pressed 'play.'

"I don't know who he was, but I didn't like it." It was Mrs. Schmidt's voice on the tape.

Phillip turned down the monitor so he could hear better.

"You're sure those are the four cards he asked about?"

"Yes, and they're the only four forgeries we have now. He must know."

"They're the only four rare ones we have too, all being sold at a great bargain. He probably wants a good deal."

"I'm nervous, Ray. Get those cards off the property. Now!"

"They're out of the store, right on top of my bureau. I'll get them off the property tomorrow."

"Tonight, Ray, please."

"You're driving me crazy! Okay, then. Later tonight. I'll take them to Ken's house. I was heading over there anyway to watch the game with him at nine. Is that all right?"

"Yes, that's fine. Thanks. I'm sorry that I'm so paranoid. One other funny thing, though. The baby monitor, the one we used to use with Luke, did you use it recently?"

"No."

"Strange. I found it under the sink behind the cabinet grille. And it was turned on. Isn't that the weirdest thing?"

"I guess."

"I put it on our bed. Doesn't it go in the carton under the bed, with all the baby stuff?"

"I think so. I'll put it back soon."

Not too soon, please, Phillip thought, thinking about Jackson hiding under the bed. She probably had it down there. He listened to another ten minutes of tape. Nothing important was said. Mrs. Schmidt had just finished preparing dinner, and they began to eat. Then the tape became blank. This must be where the batteries had run out, Phillip thought.

He turned off the cassette player and turned up the monitor. They must have finished eating a while ago. Suddenly Phillip realized that Jackson was no longer repeating her message. There was silence. Then he heard the sound of drawers being opened and closed.

"*Come here, Anne!*"

"*What is it Ray?*"

"*The cards. They were on the top of my bureau. I can't find them! Where are they?*"

"*I didn't touch them. Did you try your drawers?*"

"*Yes. They're gone!*"

"*Settle down. Now you're being paranoid. What do you think, someone just slipped in here and grabbed them while we were home?*"

That's exactly what happened, Phillip thought. That's why Jackson couldn't wait for me. He was going to get rid of the cards. She had to move fast and she did.

What should he do? He could bring the tape to the police, but by the time he did and they listened to it and were convinced that something might be wrong, it could be too late for Jackson. What if Schmidt looked under the bed for the cards? He'd find her! Phillip was terrified! He tried to imagine how scared Jackson must be. He had to do something and he had to do it now!

Chapter 23

Phillip ran as fast as he could to Art's house. He rang the bell.

"It's you again, Phillip," Mr. Norton said. "Come on in. I'll get Art."

In seconds, Art was at the front door.

"I really need your help, Art."

"What is it?"

Phillip looked at Mr. Norton, and Art said, "Dad, we'll be up in my room."

When they were in his room, Art closed the door.

"What is it, Phillip?"

"Art, Jackson's in trouble. Big trouble. It's a long story and I don't have time to explain. She's trapped in a house with criminals."

"Phillip," Art said with doubting eyes. He remembered the sawed bat and also Phillip's false murder accusation.

"You have to trust me, Art!"

"Why don't you call the police?"

"By the time I convinced them, it might be too late. She's hiding under a bed, and a guy is searching the house for something. We have no time! It might be too late already!"

"Okay, Phillip. I have to trust you. What do you want me to do?"

"Art, I want you to call Cards and Comics Superstore. Ask for Ray. Tell him that you have the four cards, and that if he wants them back to meet you at Andrews Field in fifteen minutes. Tell him that he must bring his wife, too. If he asks about his kid, tell him you don't care. They can take him or not. Suggest they leave him in front of a video. But be sure to tell him that they both must be there, or no cards."

"I don't understand, Phillip."

"I'll tell you everything later, Art. They'll probably want to know what you want for the cards. Tell them you want $1000 worth of real baseball cards if they ask. After I leave, wait three minutes before you call. I need to go back there and make sure they leave. Got it?"

"Yeah, Phillip, I do. You can count on me."

"I know. Thanks. See ya."

"See ya. And Phillip?"

"Yeah?"

"Good luck."

Phillip was off again. The sky was almost black now, and he ran into the garage and collected the cassette player and the monitor. Phillip then ran into the bushes and waited. It was a long few minutes. He couldn't get Jackson out of his mind. He badly wanted to turn on the monitor and see if she was all right, but he couldn't chance it. Phillip heard a sound. The side door opened. He heard quiet talking.

"I told you there was a problem!" Mrs. Schmidt stated angrily.

"Shut up, Jean! I-told-you-so's won't do any good now."

"You're sure that Luke is okay in front of the TV?"

"Yes. I locked the door with the dead bolt from the outside. He can't get out, unless he can find the key and knows how to use it."

They went into the garage. Phillip heard the slams from two car doors being shut. Next, the garage door opened, and the red Mustang drove off as the garage door automatically closed.

Phillip left the recorder and monitor on the ground, and ran around the shop to the side door. Please let this door be open. It was! Phillip knew where the light switch was now and he flicked on the lights. He scrambled up the stairs and heard a kid video blaring in the background. Phillip banged on the door and yelled, "Jackson, it's me!"

No answer. About twenty seconds later he heard her cry through the door, "Phillip!"

"Gummy bears! More gummy bears!" Luke wailed when he heard Jackson.

"Jackson, they're gone. They'll probably be gone for a little while. But they locked the door from the outside. You need to find the key, or get out through a window."

"Where's the key?"

"I don't know. Where would a guy keep a key?"

"I don't know, Phillip."

"Then there's not time to look."

"Wait, I have an idea," Jackson said. "Luke, where does your mommy and daddy keep keys?" she called into the other room.

"Wait till it's over," Luke called back from his TV chair.

Phillip heard Jackson walk across the room and the TV went off.

"Show me now, brat!" she ordered.

Phillip just sat outside the door, listening. Finally, Jackson said, "No luck. He has a collection of toy keys. We have to try something else."

"TV!" Luke screamed.

The TV was turned back on and Luke was quiet.

"Is there rope or something that you could tie up there and climb down? It's only about fifteen feet high."

"I'll check."

More waiting.

"No rope. There might be some somewhere, but it'll take too long to look. Any other ideas, Phillip?"

"I saw a guy tie sheets together to make a rope and escape from a jail on TV once. Luke probably has that video."

"This is no time to joke around, Phillip!"

"Sorry. I can't think. What else can we do? Let's see. Hey, look out the window. See if you can jump."

Phillip heard Jackson walk across the room, then return.

"No way, Phillip! I could get killed."

"I thought so. Think, Jackson!"

"I've been thinking. I did a lot of thinking under that bed! I think it's time to call the police. You have the tape and I have the cards. I didn't think that the tape was enough, not after the Robert Hallman thing. With the cards too, we have the extra evidence we need."

The police, of course! "Do it, Jackson."

Jackson went to the phone. Phillip could hear her through the door.

"Is Detective Stokes there, or Officer Hardwick?"

Pause.

"This is Jackson Curcio...Yes, this is an emergency! I'm at the apartment above Cards and Comics Superstore, the Schmidt's home. I'm in serious trouble. I'm trapped here. And they left their four year old kid here alone. Just get here! Send Hardwick or Stokes if you can!" Jackson commanded.

She walked back to the door.

"Let's hope they don't get back in the next couple minutes."

"Jackson, how did you get into there in the first place?"

"I heard them all watching TV. I hoped that the door was unlocked. Most people keep doors unlocked when they're home. I was right. I knew I could sneak into their bedroom without being seen. I needed to get those cards before they got rid of them. They were the evidence we needed. While I was in the bedroom, the Schmidts went back into the kitchen. And I knew they'd see me from there if I tried to leave. I found the monitor on the bed, so I took it underneath with me and I just kept repeating the message for you."

"How did you know I'd come?"

"I figured you would when you couldn't find me at home. And what else could I do? I had nothing to lose."

"They could have heard you."

"It seemed worth the risk," Jackson answered.

Phillip heard cars stop outside the shop. He saw flashing blue lights reflect up the stairway.

Four police officers trotted up the stairs. Cable was leading the way, followed by a young guy Phillip had never seen. Then came Detective Stokes and Officer Hardwick. Yes!

"Not you again!" Cable roared at Phillip.

Detective Stokes ignored Cable. "What is it son?" he asked.

"Jackson's trapped in there. The Schmidts are crooks!"

"Slow down Phillip," Detective Stokes said. "Go on."

"They sell fake cards and signed shirts and things. I have evidence. Jackson has four fake cards, and I have a tape of their conversations. They talk about selling their fake stuff and worry about getting caught."

"Their signed shirts are fake?" Cable cursed. "I paid seventy-five bucks to get my kid a signed Derek Jeter uniform here! I'll be a son-of-a-...That dirty creep!"

"Where's the tape?" Officer Hardwick asked.

"In the bushes in the back yard," Phillip answered.

"I'll go check," the new officer said, and went down the stairs.

"Jackson," Detective Stokes called from outside the door, "is the kid away from the doorway?"

"Yes."

"Get away yourself too. I'm busting in."

"Let me," Cable said. "Nothing would make me happier than to bust that thieving crook's door down. A phony Derek Jeter! I never saw my kid so happy. Now I have to break the news to him."

Cable took a few steps back and ran into the door, shoulder first. Bam! The door moved a little but didn't open. Cable tried again. No luck.

"Damn! My shoulder!"

"Let me give it a shot," Detective Stokes said.

It looks much easier on TV, Phillip thought. It took two times for Detective Stokes to bust through. Jackson and Luke were in the corner, standing wide-eyed watching everyone barge in.

"Phillip!" Jackson screamed and ran over and hugged him. She hadn't done that since they were six, but he didn't mind. He was so happy to see her sparkling face.

The new police officer walked in and handed Cable the cassette player.

"Jackson, give them the cards," Phillip said.

Jackson reached into her pocket and pulled out four cards. There was a 1961 Roger Maris, a 1948 Ted Williams, a Mickey Mantle rookie card and a Henry Aaron rookie card. It said Hank Aaron. That's what they called him back then. She handed them to Detective Stokes.

Suddenly, Jean Schmidt came running up the stairs. "Luke, Luke!" she cried. "Is he all right."

"He's fine," Jackson said.

"You?" she asked. "What are you doing here?"

"What's going on?" Ray Schmidt asked, running up the stairs.

"Mr. and Mrs. Schmidt, have a seat," Cable ordered.

"Are we under arrest?" Ray Schmidt asked.

"You will be if you don't sit down! Phillip, play us all that tape of yours."

Everyone stared at the cassette player as Phillip rewound the tape and pressed 'play.'

"You're sure those are the four cards he asked about?"

"Yes, and they're the only four forgeries we have now. He must know."

"They're the only four rare ones we have too, all being sold at a great bargain. He probably wants a good deal."

"I'm nervous, Ray. Get those cards off the property. Now!"

"They're out of the store, right on top of my bureau. I'll get them off the property tomorrow."

"Tonight, Ray, please."

Detective Cable turned off the cassette player and said, "I think we've heard enough. Mr. and Mrs. Schmidt, you're under arrest."

CHAPTER 24

Phillip stepped up to the plate. The fans in the Braves section of the stands gave a big cheer. Phillip was filled with pride. Even though he was the number nine hitter, he was actually a starter. It was the first time all season that he had started!

George Ramirez was pitching for the Pharmacy. The game was in the bottom of the third, and no Brave hitter had reached base safely yet. Eight up, eight down. Boy would I like to spoil this guy's perfect game, Phillip thought. Ramirez didn't throw hard but he had a great curve ball. Most kids this age who threw curves had a hard time throwing it over the plate consistently, but Ramirez was picking his spots today. The Pharmacy had a 1-0 lead.

"Let's go, Phil!" Mike roared from the stands. Mike had told Phillip that he should start calling himself Phil instead of Phillip. What major leaguer was ever called Phillip? Phil Plantier, Phil Rizzutto, Phil Garner. But no Phillips that Mike knew of. Phillip had argued that he didn't feel like a Phil, he felt like a Phillip, but he had said that it was okay for Mike to call him Phil at a game. It couldn't hurt and might help. Psychology and confidence were key ingredients in baseball.

The other Braves on the bench exchanged glances and mostly laughed. They didn't think of Phillip as a Phil either.

"Let's go Phil, you can do it!" Art screamed. "He's no pitcher. You're a hitter, Phil. You're a hitter!"

The other kids looked at Art. Art stood there, tall, muscular, intense, and totally absorbed in the game. He was not making fun of Phillip. He was dead serious. Art was always dead serious about baseball.

"You're the man, Phil, you're the man!" Lars chanted.

"Do it, Phil, do it!" Harry called.

More baseball chatter. The whole team was cheering 'Phil' on.

Phillip got the sign from the coach. Green light. Phillip smiled. He'd go after the first pitch. Ramirez had started out with a curve on seven of the first eight batters. George Ramirez wound up and pitched. It was sailing in very slowly. Phillip was sure that he was going to wallop it. He took a big swing. He missed. Strike one. Phillip had never seen a pitch curve that much! Wow! The next two pitches came in just as slowly and Phillip missed each by just as much. A strike out. Three outs.

"Way to take those swings, Phil," Art said.

"Good job," the other kids said. "Nice try."

Phillip jogged out to right field for the top of the fourth. It was a beautiful sunny Sunday afternoon, a perfect day for the final game of the season. Art Norton was pitching for the Pizza House Braves. He had pitched almost as well as Ramirez. A walk, a passed ball by Lars and a throwing error by Harry had accounted for the only Pharmacy run. The game had the makings of a classic.

Art struck out the first two Pharmacy batters. Charly Cable came to the plate. Batting third in the line-up, Charly was their shortstop, and one of their best hitters. Art pitched cautiously and quickly fell behind two balls and no strikes. Both pitches were outside curves. On the 2-0 pitch, Art threw a fastball. Cable swung and hit a bouncing shot towards the gap in right center. Phillip raced over as fast as he could and tried to get in front of it. He was just about in position when the ball hopped and came straight at his face! Phillip tried to move, but it was too late. Whack, right in the nose! He felt pain like he had never felt before. He badly wanted to get the ball, but looking around made him dizzy, and he fell to the ground. He felt something warm and wet below his nose, then tasted that saltiness of blood in his mouth. He just lay on his back while he heard screaming and running in the background.

"Throw it!" someone yelled.

Phillip just kept his eyes closed. Minutes seemed to pass.

"Are you all right?" Phillip opened his eyes. It was Mike standing over him.

"Yeah, I think so. What happened?"

"Inside the park home run. There was a play at the plate, but Lars dropped the ball. Cable was safe."

The whole Brave team was crowding around Phillip, seeing if he was all right, and trying to see how gross it was, too. Blood on the baseball diamond was always a good next-day topic of conversation.

"Clear away!" a husky voice boomed. Phillip's teammates backed off. It was Detective Cable. "You okay?"

Phillip nodded.

"Phillip, that play took guts. You got your face right down where it was supposed to be. My Stuart is a hell of an athlete, but if he had your brains and balls, he'd be the best. Nice play."

Coach Higgins edged in front of Detective Cable. "Nice try, Phil. You remind me of Nomar Garciaparra with that kind of effort. Can you get up?"

"Yeah," Phillip said as he tried to stand. He felt the blood start to run down his face again. Did he really play like Nomar Garciaparra? Phillip thought of Nomar as the leader of the Boston Red Sox. His headfirst slides and diving catches made him one of the most intense players in all of professional baseball.

"Hold this on your nose," Coach Higgins said, handing Phillip a handkerchief. "Jamien, get out here!"

Everyone cheered for Phillip as he walked to the dugout. What a day it's been, he thought as he sat on the bench. The kids had greeted him like a hero when he arrived for the game. All the kids who had bought fake stuff from Cards and Comics were getting their money back, thanks to Phillip. It was part of an agreement the police had made with the Schmidts. Also, the Schmidts had to close their shop. The Schmidts would plead guilty but only spend thirty days in jail. In exchange, Jackson would not be charged with trespassing. All of Centerville was talking about Phillip and Jackson, and about their fearless, ingenious detective work. Detective Cable had made sure that everyone knew all about it. Before today's game, some of his teammates had greeted him as 'Sleuth,' but this time they were not making fun of him. And now, even though he had struck out and was responsible for an inside-the-park Pharmacy home run, he was still treated like a hero. Despite his teary eyes and a bloody and very painful nose, this was the best day of his life.

Jay struck out to start the bottom of the fourth. Ramirez walked Harry, but Greg popped up for the second out. Lars came up, badly wanting to make amends for his two botched plays in the field. Ramirez is losing his control, Phillip thought. Give him the red light, Coach. Coach Higgins did. Ball one. Lars had the red light on the next two, and they were balls as well. Mr. Green went out to talk with his pitcher. They exchanged words while Coach Higgins gave Lars the green light on the 3-and-0 pitch. Good move, Phillip thought. Mr. Green probably told his pitcher to stay away from the curve for a while, and he had no fastball. Ramirez wound up and pitched. Smack! It was the hardest ball Lars had ever hit! It went a mile over the left field fence! The score was tied 2-2! Ramirez got Art to ground out to first for the final out.

In the fifth, both teams were retired easily. Phillip's nose had completely stopped bleeding by now. He prayed that Coach Higgins would put him back in. The one time a player could return to a game was when he or she was taken out because of an injury. But Jamien was sent out to play right in the sixth.

Art was tiring, but the first two Pharmacy batters were out on hard hit balls to the infield. Stuart Cable came up, and Art never gave him a pitch to hit. He walked him on four straight outside pitches. Tao came up next. He walked on four straight balls as well. Coach Higgins didn't say a word. It was Art's game to win or lose. Art had been the Brave's best player all spring. It was all up to him. Larry Caposella stepped up to the plate for the Pharmacy. Two men on, two out. Tie ball game. Art wound up and fired. The pitch was smacked past Maggie over first base, a fair ball. It bounced all the way to the fence where it rolled around in the corner into foul territory. Jamien saw it in foul ground and stopped running.

"Jamien!" Phillip yelled. "It's fair!"

The crowd was screaming so loud that Jamien didn't hear anyone. Doesn't he know that if it hits fair first in the outfield that it doesn't matter if it rolls foul? Stuart scored! The Pharmacy mobbed him at the plate. Tao ran into an even bigger crowd at the plate as he jumped into his teammates' arms. By the time Jamien heard the umpire calling "fair ball," Larry was rounding third and heading home. Maggie was at the fence by now. She picked up the ball and pegged it to the plate, but not in time. It was a three run home run. The Pharmacy now led, 5-2. Phillip was stunned. He had been sure that Art would get the job done. Art always did! But it struck him that something wasn't right about the play. He replayed it in his head. Then it came to him.

"Coach! Tao never touched home plate! Tell Lars!" Phillip yelled.

In the past, Coach Higgins had always ignored Phillip with things like this, but now he ran out to Lars and whispered something to him. The Pharmacy Phillies were stacked high in a pig pile at home. Lars pushed his way into the crowd, spotted Tao, and tagged him with the ball.

"Out!" the umpired ruled on the appeal play. Only one run had scored! Tao was the third out, and so Larry's run didn't count! It was still just 3-2!

The Braves now screamed and mobbed Lars at home plate. When he finally climbed out from under his team's pile of players, he said, "It was Phillip. He told Coach Higgins and Coach Higgins told me."

"All right, Phil!"

"Yeah, Phil!"

The whole team surrounded Phillip, slapping him high fives.

Jay led off the bottom of the last with an infield single. Jamien was due up, when Coach Higgins asked Phillip, "Can you pinch hit? We need a bunt here."

"Yeah," Phillip said, and he walked to the plate.

Phillip watched the first four pitches go by, the first two for balls, the third a strike, and then another ball. They were all curves. He'll throw a fastball now, Phillip thought. Give me the green light. I'll get a bunt single. Coach Higgins did give the green light. Ramirez pitched, Phillip squared to bunt. The ball was way high. Phillip started to run to first. "Strike!" sounded the umpired.

"Huh?" Phillip asked.

"You never pulled the stick back. It's a swinging strike."

How stupid, Phillip thought! You have to pull the bat back if it's a ball and you've squared to bunt! I know that!

It was 3-and-2 now. The next pitch was another fastball. Swing. Strike three. He struck out! He should have walked! Phillip trudged to the bench, feeling like he wanted to cry.

"That's all right, Phil."

"Good try, Phil."

Next, Harry struck out too. Then Greg singled Jack to third. The Braves screamed. Phillip could only think, 'It would be tied if it weren't for me.'

Lars was up with runners on first and third, two out. With a 1-and-1 count, he smashed a grounder between short and third. Stuart Cable dove and stabbed the ball, he got up, cranked his arm back and fired to first. Lars was not fast. He was out by a half a step. The game was over.

We lost, Phillip thought. And it's all my fault. He fought back tears.

Coach Higgins called the team together on the bench.

"Men," he said. Phillip wondered if he noticed that Maggie was not a 'man.' "That was one hell of a game. No one wanted that win more than I did, but you guys gave it your all. I know I've been pretty tough on you this season. I don't have tolerance for shenanigans. This is what I've been working for, gentleman. This made it all worthwhile. Cable made the defensive play of the season on that last one. They deserve it. Art, nice game. You did it for us all year. No one can do it every game. Phil, you used your eyes and your head and saved us two runs in the sixth. It was almost the difference. Lars, great hitting. Okay, guys, go shake hands."

After the handshake, Dara and Mike each gave Phillip a big hug. Behind them was Jake along with Jackson and the entire Curcio family.

"That was awesome," Jackson said. The rest of her family echoed Jackson's praise. Then Jake stepped forward.

"Phillip, what can I say?" Jake said. "That was a great game. I loved watching every second of it. And thanks, Phillip, for everything."

"You're not going to retire now, I hope? They didn't lease your store out to anyone else, yet, did they?"

"Actually, they did. Another drug store signed the lease Thursday. I'm out in three weeks."

"No, Jake! Then we were too slow!" Phillip cried.

"Not exactly," Jackson said, holding her lips together to hide a smile, but her joyful eyes gave her away.

"That's right," Jake said. "It seems that there is a vacant store property right where Cards and Comics Superstore used to be. I hear two hot shot detectives cracked a case of criminal forgery, and those guys are out of business. That store is bigger than my old one, but with the competition out of the way, I expect business will be booming."

Phillip grinned.

"Oh, Jake, that's great." He gave Jake a big hug.

"But there's one thing that bothers me," Jake said. "I feel bad that you won't be able to take advantage of my giant going-out-of-business sale."

"Jake, I don't care about that! I'd much rather have you, and have your store open!"

"That's nice, but here's a little something for you anyway."

Jake handed Phillip a baseball card. It was a Casey Stengel manager card! It was more than thirty years old!

"Thanks, Jake." Even though he had lost the ball game and struck out twice, this was the best day of his life.

CHAPTER 25

"Colonel Mustard did it, in the drawing room, with a knife," Phillip said sitting up straight on the living room rug.

"I think you got me," Dara conceded from across the board, and smiled.

Phillip picked up the three cards from the side of the board and looked at them. He nodded to his mother.

"That's what I thought. Good game, Phillip."

"Thanks, Mom."

"Look, Emily wants to play," laughed Phillip. Emily was lying on her baby mat on the floor near the game. She was reaching toward the board.

"Keep those pieces away from her, Phillip. She'll choke on them. I'll give her these instead."

Dara reached for a rubber elephant and a red ball and handed them to Emily.

"Mr. Elephant did it with a rubber ball in the living room, Emily," Phillip said to his baby sister.

Emily laughed.

"She likes Clue, Mom!"

"She's destined to grow up to be a cracker-jack detective, I guess. It must run in the family."

"Game over?" Mike asked, putting down the Sunday sports section.

145

"Yes," Dara said. "You'll never guess who won."

Mike knew.

"Phillip, I can't tell you how proud of you I was at the game today."

"Thanks, Mike, but I struck out twice and let Cable get a home run on a hit to me. What are you so proud of?"

"Your attitude, Phillip. That's all anyone can ask of a guy. You gave 100% in that game. You got down in front of that Cable shot, just like I taught you. You got a bad break on the hop and paid the price."

"But what about my strikeouts?"

"You did your best, and besides, you saved two runs with your head on the home run appeal play. That meant as much as Lars's two run homer."

"But I'll never be really good at baseball, like Art, right?"

Mike breathed deeply and was silent. He was struggling to find the right words.

"That's all right, Mike," Phillip said. "I know I'll never be that good, and I don't mind. I just love the game."

"Phillip, you taught *me* something today."

"What?"

"Brains can be just as important as athletic skill. Even on a baseball diamond. You might be a great manager some day."

"But Mike, do you think that I can be a decent player if I work hard? With more practice, bunting is something I know I can do well. And if you keep on hitting me fungoes, I think I can be as good as Jay in the outfield."

"No question," Mike assured him.

The phone rang. Dara got up off the floor with Emily in her arms, and answered the phone.

"Hello?"

Pause.

"Just a minute," Dara said, and turned to Phillip. "It's Jackson."

"Hi, Jackson," Phillip said.

"Hi, Phil."

"Jackson, I'm Phillip. Maybe Phil at a baseball game, but I'm Phillip the rest of the time."

"Just kidding, Phillip. I was just wondering where you were for dinner. You even missed dessert tonight! We had chocolate cream pie."

"I was playing Clue with my mom. And just hanging out."

"Things sound good."

"They are," Phillip answered. "You were right."

"Hey, Phillip, I have to show you this neat card that Jake gave me. It's a card of Joanne Harris. She was a star in the women's baseball league in the 40's, the one they organized while a lot of the men were fighting World War II. Isn't that neat?"

"That's awesome, Jackson."

"Your game this afternoon was so exciting, I'm thinking of playing next season."

"That would be great! You'd be awesome!"

"Not really. I haven't played much. But maybe Mike could work with me too."

"Oh, yeah!"

"Well, I'll see ya, Phillip."

"Yeah, bye." Phillip hung up the phone.

Emily was propped up in her sit-up seat on the floor. She had dropped her cloth diaper and now she was fussing.

"Phillip, can you hand her the spit rag?" Dara asked.

Phillip picked up the diaper and tossed it towards Emily. It hit her in the face, and she laughed. Phillip grabbed the diaper from her and threw it in her face again. She exploded in a belly laugh.

"Look Mom! Look Mike! She's playing catch with me! She likes baseball!"

Phillip grabbed the diaper once more, and looked toward Emily, pretending that he was a pitcher. He waved off the first sign. He waved off the second. Then he nodded.

"The wind up, and the pitch..." Phillip said. He pitched the diaper at Emily. "Fastball. Strike two!"

Emily laughed uncontrollably as the cloth diaper opened up and covered her whole face.

Mike and Dara laughed too.

"Want to play a little baseball now, Phillip?" Mike asked.

"In a few minutes, Dad, um, I mean Mike. We're in the middle of a batter."

Phillip held the diaper and looked towards Emily. He got a sign and nodded. Emily giggled.

"He winds up," Phillip announced to Emily, "he pitches...strike three!"

Emily laughed again.

"Good at bat, Emily," Phillip said as he jumped up and ran upstairs to his bedroom.

In his room, Phillip grabbed his glove from on top of his bed. He slid his left hand into the soft leather mitt and pounded it twice with his right fist. He looked up and nodded to Nomar Garciaparra. The brand new poster was taped up on the ceiling next to Tony LaRussa.

"I hope you don't mind a little company," Phillip said to LaRussa. The former Oakland manager looked down at Phillip and seemed to nod okay.

Phillip turned around and ran downstairs to play ball.

ABOUT THE AUTHOR

Mark Fidler lives in Waltham, Massachusetts with his wife and three sons. Besides teaching high school math and computer science, he has coached youth hockey and Little League baseball.

Also written by Mark Fidler—

Pond Puckster, an exciting and moving hockey story!

For more information about *Pond Puckster* as well as new books soon to be published, visit the author's web page at

www.markfidler.com

To purchase *Pond Puckster*, call Customer Service toll-free at (877) 823-9235 or visit the bookstore at

iUniverse.com

Also sold through most .com bookstores

How did you like Baseball Sleuth?
Tell the author! Email him at author@markfidler.com